What Our Storms Create

K. R. Vanderport

Contents

Snow Angels in the Road

For Dad

1.

All he could see was white. Brighter than the sun. He squinted against it and tried to get his bearings.

After a storm like the one they'd had, looking for the lines on the roads was an exercise in futility. The only clue they had to which part of the fluffy expanse was pavement and which was field was the tracks left by other cars. Ken followed them and hoped whoever had come before hadn't ended up in a ditch.

In an environment that had more in common with a blank piece of printer paper than the earth it had buried, anything that might have gone unnoticed suddenly drew the eye as well as any neon sign could. At first, when it was a speck in the distance, Ken thought it was a small boulder. He wondered if they'd been driving through a field after all. As he got closer, though, it became clear that it was more of a lump than a true obstacle. There were tire tracks going completely over it.

One heartbeat pounded heavily inside his chest, like it was trying to get his attention. Ken slowed down.

"What's that?" Mary asked. She leaned forward and squinted through the windshield. "It looks like a pile of clothes. Did someone leave their laundry on the road?"

His wife's glasses prescription was lower, so it took Ken another few yards to make out the clothes. He pressed harder on the brakes, and the car jerked to a stop. He put it in park and unlocked his seatbelt.

"Ken?"

"Wait here a second," he said. "I'm just going to move it out of the road."

"Don't fall," she warned. "If you fall, I'll have to come try to help you up. Then I'll fall, and we'll both be piles of laundry in the road."

Ken smirked, but made sure to place his boots carefully. He made his way over to the clothes. They'd clearly been there for a while. The tire tracks only showed up because of the snow that had fallen on the pile, and a new dusting was now beginning to cover the tracks themselves. It was odd, though; the clothes were laid out in a straight line, in the order they would be in if someone was wearing them.

He knelt down and brushed the snow off the hooded jacket. It wasn't stiff yet and moved with his touch. Ken had never been hit by a sledgehammer before, but he imagined it felt similar to the moment when he realized it wasn't a pile of clothes in the road; it was a child.

Ken tore his glove off and felt the child's neck. Miraculously, his fingers found a faint pulse. He started brushing the rest of the snow off, mind racing. The child was only wearing a hoodie, jeans, and some thin, good for nothing gloves. They didn't even have shoes on; just socks covering their little feet.

His first instinct was to call an ambulance, but eighty years of life experience took hold of him and shook him out of his panic. The hospital was half an hour away. If an ambulance left immediately, the child wouldn't be warm for half an hour and wouldn't get real medical help for twice that.

Moving an injured body, especially one that had been run over by a car – and yes, the fact that the snow didn't immediately melt under the heat of his rage was surprising – was dangerous. He knew that. He also knew leaving a child outside in this cold, not knowing how long they had already been there, would probably prove fatal before the ambulance could make it halfway.

As gently as he could, Ken lifted the child's body and cradled it against his chest. He started back towards the car. Mary had already gotten out, worried by his reaction to the "laundry." When she saw the child, her eyes widened.

"CALL 9-1-1!" Ken shouted.

She nodded, shuffling around to the driver's side of the car. By the time Ken climbed into the backseat, trying to keep from shifting the child's body too much, she was already explaining the situation to someone.

"Hang on." She grabbed a fistful of an electric blanket, shoving it towards her husband. They kept it in the car to ward off the chill as the engine warmed up. "We'll be there in fifteen or twenty minutes," she said, estimating cutting the drive time by up to half.

Ken's immediate reaction was fear that going too fast would end up with all three of them dying in a car wreck. He glanced up, meeting her eyes in the rearview mirror. She nodded at him. He nodded back and finished wrapping the child in the electric blanket. Mary had experience driving quickly during emergencies. They would be fine.

As they drove, Ken studied the child in his arms. It was a boy, cheeks still rounded even though he looked malnourished. A chant he'd overheard during one of his daughter's sleepovers came to mind. He tried to shake it away – this was no time for hysteria.

"It's going to be okay," he whispered to the boy.

Light as a feather, stiff as a board, his brain chanted. The barely restrained glee in the childish voices of his memories grated on his nerves. Especially because he couldn't contradict their words.

Light as a feather, stiff as a board.

Light as a feather, stiff as a board.

Light as a feather, stiff as a board.

2.

Memorizing the route to the pediatric intensive care unit hadn't been something Ken and Mary had wanted to do, but it was coming in handy now. As soon as they arrived, a flurry of scrubs and long, white coats took the boy's body from Ken's arms and put him down on a stretcher. Before he could open his mouth, Ken was standing with his wife in an empty hallway, holding only an electric blanket.

He looked down at it, noticing for the first time that the electric cord was trailing behind him like a tail. With the blue plaid pattern, it was easy to make out the dark stains of blood on the fabric. Ken balled it up and shoved it in the nearest trash can.

Mary was the one who approached the nurse's desk, where a bored young man swiveled back and forth in an office chair.

"Hello, we're here with that little boy who just came in. He got run over."

Ken shuddered involuntarily, disgust and horror mixing together inside his chest and monopolizing the air in his lungs.

"Yes, alright. Just take this and fill the form out." The nurse didn't even blink at the mention of a child getting run over. It wasn't clear if that was evidence of his mental fortitude or an indication that the world was a much more depraved place than expected.

Mary walked with her husband to the waiting area, but left as he sat down. He wasn't sure where she was going, looking instead at all the blanks he had no idea how to fill. He put himself down as the primary contact. Circling all the questions about the boy, he drew an arrow he hoped the nurse would recognize as a sign to flip the page over. He didn't know his name, but what he did know, he wrote down.

Young boy, approx. 5-8 years. Blond hair, pale skin. Run over by unknown vehicle. Found in red hoodie, blue jeans, black gloves, white socks. Approx. 3-4 ft. Only moved to put his head on my shoulder...

Ken cursed quietly and scribbled out the last sentence. Mary was standing over him again, like an angel appearing and disappearing as she pleased. She took the clipboard out of his hands and gave him a fistful of wet paper towels instead.

As she headed back to the desk to return the form, he stared after her and wondered what the towels were for. When he finally looked down, he felt sick. Once warm and red, the mess on his hands was now brown and dry. He did his best to wipe the blood off, but even when he couldn't see it, he could feel it. He dropped the paper towels to the floor, too exhausted to find a trash can.

Mary kicked them under their chairs and out of sight before sitting down. She took his hand and massaged the back of it with her thumb.

"We were going to your mom's," Ken said. "I'm sorry."

"Don't be. I called Liam; he's going to go over there and get the mail, take the garbage out, all that fun stuff."

He huffed a laugh. "He's a good boy."

"Yes, he is." She smiled. "We did well with him."

Of course, Liam wasn't a boy like the one in surgery; their youngest son was almost twenty-five years old. He worked as a game designer for some major company and volunteered at doggie daycare on the weekends just for fun. Though he was the reason his parents were well acquainted with pediatric intensive care, he had grown up into a strong, confident, and independent young man. Ken hoped this new boy would get the chance to do the same.

~

If worry and anticipation actually spurred surgeries on, they'd be over before they'd begun. As it is, minutes and hours bend and stretch, one person sleeping while others sit in bland, symmetrical rooms with plants that don't even have the decency to grow, if only to prove that time is still moving. The one in surgery is never the only one hanging in an artificially suspended state of being.

There's nothing you can do in times like those. Everything is boring or irritating. Anything that would usually bring someone joy mocks them with endorphins that clash garishly against the background of the situation. Distractions are guilt-ridden and pointless, only serving to amplify the utter helplessness that caused them to be sought out.

"Hey, I'm back," Mary said. She sat down next to her husband, careful not to spill what she was holding.

He blinked at the spoils with confusion. She was holding a bag of food and a drink carrier from a fast food place down the street. For a moment, he'd forgotten there was anything outside the hospital. He shook his head.

"'m not hungry."

"You need to eat something," she insisted. "The doctors are going to kick you out if you starve yourself."

"They won't notice," he countered.

"They will if I tell them." She held out the bag of food.

He took it with a sigh. "Thank you."

She nodded, settling down and helping him separate the food. She took a sip of her drink and studied him. It took him longer to notice than usual, but eventually he caught on.

"What?" He asked.

"Nothing. It's just…" She took another sip and set the drink off to the side. "You haven't been on this end of things since Liam was little, have you?"

He frowned, searching his memory. "There was that time when you got your gall bladder removed."

"Okay, so one time in the last – what is it now? Twenty years?"

"I guess so," he said. "I'm sorry you've had to go through all that."

She shook her head. "That's not it; I'm just saying you're out of practice. You forgot that you have to take care of yourself right now if you want to be able to help anyone later."

He sighed. "I guess so."

She smoothed the creases in his forehead with her finger, smiling fondly. "That's okay. I got you."

It took another few hours, but eventually an exhausted-looking doctor came looking for them. Mary had been reading to Ken, who was still too impatient to do that himself. Constantly monitoring the traffic around them, she stopped in the middle of a sentence when a white lab coat didn't veer off course like the others. They stood up together.

Ken's first thought was the same as whenever he met so-called professionals these days; I can't believe they trusted a kid to do this. She was somewhere between his second and third children in age.

"Are you the ones who brought the John Doe boy in? The one who was run over?" She asked. When they nodded, she continued. "I'm Doctor Raina Ortega; I operated on him and I'll be overseeing his care until...for the foreseeable future."

"How is he?" Ken asked.

"He's alive," she answered. "But there was a lot of damage. I don't know if he'll make it through the next few days, and even if he does, there's only a small chance he'll ever regain consciousness."

Ken swallowed hard. As Mary's hand slipped into his, he asked, "Can we see him?"

The doctor shifted. "It's against policy to let anyone who isn't immediate family see a patient in this critical a condition."

"Have you found any immediate family?"

"I have some nurses looking into it."

"But have you found anyone?"

Ortega pursed her lips. "No."

Ken seemed to radiate a commanding atmosphere. Usually, he was incredibly gentle and kind, but there were times when he seemed to pull that atmosphere tighter to himself and justify everyone's instinctive initial reaction to him. His voice even seemed to get deeper and stronger. Most people who didn't know him, and even some who did, described it as "scary." It wasn't that he was yelling or even trying to intimidate them; it was just the effect of what his wife called his "power of presence."

Mary was never afraid of him, not even when he got passionate about something like he was at that moment. What felt threatening to strangers felt comfortable to her, because she knew him. Holding his hand as his emotion tapped into that power, she felt his presence wrap around her like a shield.

"Look, Dr. Ortega," he was saying. "That little boy can't be more than seven years old. He might be dying, and if – God forbid – he does, I don't want him to be alone. I want him to know someone..." he took a second to swallow his grief. "...someone cares about him."

Ortega had grown up around a lot of lying, manipulative, and traitorous people. She'd been planning on going into psychology, but it had opened too many old wounds for her. So, she'd become a surgeon. It was a way for her to keep her distance from repeats of her history, but still be the kind of help she'd needed as a kid. Of all the doctors in the hospital, she was the one they needed. She saw Ken's strength for what it was, and she cared more about her patients than she did about the rules.

"Okay," she said. "But you have to stay out of the way if anything goes wrong."

"Of course." Ken nodded.

"Thank you," Mary said.

Ortega dropped them off in a sterile room with "John Doe" scribbled in blue marker on a clipboard-sized whiteboard nailed to the door. The only things that distinguished the boy as an individual were the readings on his charts. Ken pulled a chair over next to the bed, and Mary pulled one up next to him.

For the next four hours of her shift, Ortega checked in as often as she could. The two were almost always in the same position, as if they'd decided the boy needed a pair of stone guardians watching over him. She checked in one last time before clocking out. Ken and Mary told her to drive safely and thanked her again, but didn't make any move to leave.

~

Ken had four children in total; two with his high school sweetheart, and two with his sweet Mary. All the nights he'd stayed up to watch over one of them, all the times he'd promised to sit right there and keep them safe while they slept, probably totaled up to at least a fourth of his life.

Most of the time, he'd ended up falling asleep, too. Then again, most of the time, thank God, they hadn't been in a hospital. He wasn't sure he'd ever slept when one of his kids was in the hospital, and he wasn't about to break that streak now. He was a light sleeper, anyway, so all the sounds in the halls, other rooms, and over the PA system inadvertently helped him.

Mary had left to get some coffee. Afraid of not being allowed back in if she left the building, she'd gone in search of a kiosk or a break room of some sort. She'd taken her phone, promising to text him if she got caught so he wouldn't be worried.

The boy looked even smaller than he had in the car, somehow. His tiny body was covered in bandages, and he had a ridiculous amount of IV's attached to him. Ken hadn't known there were that many different fluids in the human body. The hospital blanket was pulled up to his shoulders, but one of his little hands stuck out the side.

Ken tried to move it under the blanket, but the boy's fingers suddenly tightened. Ken's heartbeat stumbled, lungs forgetting momentarily what they were supposed to do. His pointer finger was trapped in a diminutive fist. It was the first time the boy had moved since he'd gotten out of surgery.

Ken looked around, wondering if he should call the nurses and whether he could do that without accidentally pulling away. He was not going to let go of the boy's hand. Whatever the child had been through, he still had enough innocence in him to reach back when someone reached out to him. Ken was not going to break that trust.

The boy didn't move again, so he settled into his chair and started rubbing the back of the tiny hand with his thumb.

"It's okay," he whispered to the boy. "I'm here."

Love is the most unpredictable and irrational thing in the universe. It side-steps any attempt to quantify it and laughs in the face of all who try to break it down to a formula. More chaotic than entropy, more constant than gravity, and more powerful than time itself, it's unpredictably unpredictable.

Some parents love their children the instant they set eyes on them. Some parents only ever love themselves. One couple might get married after two weeks and stay together till death do them part, while another two people might be friends for decades before ever considering each other in a romantic way.

Someone had been cruel enough to toss the boy out of their car in the middle of a frozen Minnesota day, regardless of what history they'd shared. Ken didn't know the color of the boy's eyes or the sound of his voice, but he loved him all the same.

Over the next four days, Ken ate with one hand and only left the boy to go to the bathroom. The aluminum bar on the bed grew warm under his arm.

Mary brought him food and clean clothes. After thirty-six hours, she made him sleep. He didn't reclaim his finger even for that, instead rearranging himself and his chair so he could make sure the boy knew he was there, even when he was unconscious.

The longest power nap he took was four hours. He couldn't bear to leave the kid alone any longer. He watched the rise and fall of the boy's chest, listening to the strangled way he breathed even with an oxygen mask on. Ken found himself falling in sync with the boy, heart beating frantically in the time between breaths. He was constantly afraid that each one would be the child's last.

Every morning, when Ortega came in, she seemed surprised the boy made it through the night. She checked him over, changed his fluids and bandages, and translated the charts for Ken and Mary. Every day, she told them the same thing; the chances of his survival were slim, and he still might never wake up again. The boy either couldn't hear her or didn't care, because he kept living. He hung onto Ken's finger and survived.

3.

On the morning of the fourth day, the boy opened his eyes. When Ken raised his gaze from his book and saw them, he almost had a heart attack. He heard Mary gasp and hurry to the door, yelling for a nurse. He and the boy just looked at each other.

"Hello." He fought the urge to completely collapse into tears. "My name is Ken. I'm here to take care of you."

The boy's eyes were a little glassy, confused. His fist tightened around Ken's finger, and when he spoke his voice was almost inaudible. "I'm Cody," he said.

Ortega was on her way out when she heard her name over the PA system. She recognized the boy's room number immediately and felt her pulse stutter. Only her dedication to professionalism kept her from sprinting back up the stairs and down the hall.

Before she even got there, grief was choking her. She'd lost patients before, of course, but Ken and Mary hadn't. If she'd been more irrational, she would have hoped they hadn't been there when it happened. But she was never one to hide from the truth, and she knew Ken wouldn't have left the boy's side.

When she entered the room, she was startled to see the boy's eyes open. His little hand was completely engulfed in Ken's larger ones, and the nurses did their best to work around that. In the three steps it took her to get over to the bed, Ortega got herself back under control.

"Hey," she put a hand on Ken's shoulder. "I'm going to need you to move for a minute."

Ken nodded, patting the boy's hand. "I'll be right over there, okay?"

The boy nodded.

"Thank you," Ortega smiled.

Ken gave her a small smile in return. "His name's Cody," he said. "He doesn't remember his last name."

"Okay." She surveyed the situation and decided they could manage with one less nurse. "Matisse; go check those missing persons reports again. Look for the name 'Cody.'"

Ortega checked the boy over. He was incredibly weak, which was understandable considering what he'd been through. She hadn't expected him to pull through at all, though, so she was impressed. As she worked – looking over his readings, comparing them to his charts, asking him questions – she noticed that he kept looking back at Ken.

The man stood at the end of the bed, arms crossed, looking like a guardian angel. Ortega almost asked him to say, "Do not be afraid" to her nurses. She wasn't sure if he would have heard her, though. He seemed oblivious to everything going on around him. He was just watching Cody, as if the boy was the only person in the whole world.

~

"You need to get some rest," Mary said. "You don't sleep well in the hospital. You never have."

Ken shook his head. "I'm not leaving Cody alone in a strange place the first night after he woke up."

The two of them were sitting in the cafeteria. Ortega had taken Cody off to do some more in-depth tests, promising to let them know as soon as they brought him back. They'd decided to be daring and order dessert, even though hospital food had a reputation for a reason. Either this particular hospital was the exception to the rule or Cody waking up had triggered some sort of psychosomatic response, because even the plastic-wrapped egg salad sandwiches tasted delicious.

"Okay, but you've probably gotten less than twelve hours of sleep over the past couple days. You're going to burn out pretty soon, and then you'll be of no use to Cody." Some of Mary's sandwich escaped out the side, and she licked her fingers clean. "You can come right back in the morning."

Ken's forehead creased. "He's too young to be here alone."

Mary sighed. "How about this; we'll set up shifts."

"You've barely had more sleep than me—"

"Not just with us," she interrupted. "Liam can help out, and Esther can come on the weekends."

"I don't want them to have to do that," he said.

"They'd be happy to help," Mary assured him. "And it's not like they'd have to stay here for twenty-four hours straight. That's what the shifts would be for."

Liam lived in town and his immediate older sister, Esther, taught English a few hours away. She drove down every couple weekends and had even been known to come for a few hours on a school night if it was a special occasion. She liked to brag about how the drive was "nothing" to her anymore. The older two would have been happy to help, but they lived almost four hours away.

"I want to be the one with him," Ken admitted.

She looked at him, straight through his eyes and into his mind. "If this is going to work, you have to let us help you."

He sighed. "Alright," he said. "You can all take turns while I'm sleeping, but I'm doing the rest of the time."

"I would have expected nothing else." Mary smiled, then leaned in and kissed him. She was a physically affectionate person, but it was more than that. She communicated things through touch that she couldn't figure out how to phrase. For example, she kissed him; but what she was really saying was, "It's going to be okay."

4.

"Stop fidgeting," Ortega said.

Cody held himself still until she turned around, then started squirming again. He tugged at the bowtie absently. When it came undone, Ken could only try to disguise his laugh with a cough. Cody looked up at him, smiling sheepishly, and held the ends of the tie out. Ken was just leaning over to redo the knot when an authoritative voice cut through the buzz of small talk that lingered in the air.

"All rise for the honorable Judge O'Connor."

Ken stuffed the bowtie in his pocket and stood up, trying to make it look like his cane was more of an aesthetic choice than a necessary part of his life. The judge sauntered up to his desk as he finished pulling his robes over a green flannel shirt and grass-stained jeans.

"Be seated." He got comfortable in his chair and grabbed the papers, barely glancing at the courtroom. Ken could tell exactly which part of the story he was at by watching his facial expressions. Finally, O'Connor looked up.

Ken straightened in his chair. He was sure that, somewhere behind him, Mary was doing the same.

O'Connor leaned over and studied him. "Are you sure you want to do this?" He asked. "I mean, kids are a huge responsibility and you're...well, you're eighty."

"I know," Ken said, smiling. "But don't worry; people in our family are known to be long livers."

The judge shrugged. "Alright. In that case, let's get started. I believe we have a character witness?"

"Yes, Your Honor," Ken's lawyer replied. "This is Doctor Raina Ortega; she was the attending physician when the child in question was first brought in."

"By this guy?" O'Connor pointed to Ken without looking at him.

"Yes," the lawyer said.

The judge nodded and leaned back in his chair. He gestured for them to proceed with a wave of his hand.

Ken, Mary, their lawyer, and Ortega had gone over the plan something like two million five hundred and six times, so Ken knew he had a few minutes to kill before he had to start paying attention. He looked over at Cody, who was swinging his legs and twisting his jacket sleeves, completely unconcerned with his fate as only a child can be.

It was amazing how much innocence had survived in him. From what they could piece together, his life so far had not been nearly what he deserved. Cody deserved the world. He deserved to be loved and safe.

Ken had brought up the idea of adoption with Mary one night as they held each other in the dark. He'd been nervous, apologizing and saying they could still do all the things they had planned, go all the places they'd talked about. They could have one of the kids take Cody while they were gone – it could still be just the two of them every once in a while.

Mary had just laughed. "I've known he's going to be ours for a long time."

"What...?"

"Come on, honey," she had sighed, pressing their foreheads together. "Give me a little credit; I've known since that first day at the hospital."

"Really?" To be honest, he hadn't known for about a week. The stress of watching Cody struggle had overwritten all his thoughts, blocking out everything – especially obvious things, like the fact that *the* boy had become his boy.

"You're not subtle," Mary had teased.

He'd kissed her then.

After Ortega's nurses failed to find anything about Cody, they called in the police. That was not as effective as they'd hoped – they couldn't even find a birth certificate.

Cody tried to help, but he was six. He'd stayed with an "Uncle John." They'd lived in a white house, between a brown house and another white house on a street that had "lots more houses." His truck was red. The license plate had "some numbers on it, but some letters, too".

The good thing about not being able to find Cody's so-called uncle was that Ken and Mary didn't have to fight anyone for custody. Also, because they had no idea who John was, neither of them ended up in prison for justifiable homicide. The bad thing was that it took forever and a day to get through all the Himalayan mountains of paperwork that came with registering a kid in the system. Only after that was done could they adopt him.

In the end, God's timing was perfect. Cody had been cleared to leave the rehab facility the day Ken and Mary's lawyer set for finalizing the adoption. They had to bring him back once a week for the time being, but the physical therapist told them Cody was improving so quickly it wouldn't be long before he was able to cut back to once every two weeks.

It had really been something, helping him through physical therapy. They cheered him on as he struggled, dried his tears when he wanted to give up, and told him stories as the nurses helped him get situated in bed at the end of the day. The rehabilitation home existed outside of time; a place where he could have a microcosm of a do-over childhood. Though he was bigger than any of their other children had been when learning to walk, Ken still held onto him whenever he lifted up his little hands.

It was actually nice that he was taller, Ken had mentioned to Mary. That way, he didn't have to wreck his back when helping Cody out.

"Ken?"

He looked up, drawn back into the present by his lawyer's voice.

"Are you ready?" The lawyer asked.

Ken nodded, standing. He wasn't worried anymore; Cody was already his. The judge would have no choice but to agree. Ken knew he was older – maybe the oldest man the judge had ever seen petition to adopt a child. That didn't matter. It wasn't how long a group of people were together that made them a family; it was how much they loved each other.

Of course, he wanted to live long enough to see Cody grow up. It just wasn't something he was concerned about. The boy fit into his heart like a piece he hadn't known was missing from the puzzle, and he knew this was what God wanted. In the end, there were really no decisions to be made; just facts to be accepted.

Life would happen, and when it did, Cody would be able to face it knowing he had been loved.

5.

All he could see was white. Brighter than the sun. He squinted against it and tried to get his bearings.

"Why did they change the colors of the gowns again?" Ken asked Mary in the type of stage-whisper only ninety-two-year-olds can get away with.

Just as she had the last five times he'd asked, she shrugged. "Because Maggie Prescott declared it the season's hottest color – I don't know!"

"Those kids who are renting theirs have probably had to starve all day," he mused. "Can't eat with that on; they'd spill on themselves for sure."

"That would be an embarrassing thing to have preserved for posterity on each of the twelve thousand videos around here," she agreed.

"Well, when we watch the eleven thousand you took," he teased, "we'll have to look for that."

"Sorry, the line for the bathroom was insane," Raina Ortega said as she made her way over, adjusting the bracelets on her arms.

"Don't worry; we haven't even seen him yet," Mary reassured her.

Cody's graduating class had around four hundred kids in it. They moved around in the crowd, white caps and gowns drawing the eye, almost painful in the florescent lights. It seemed odd that there were that many kids the same age as Cody. The boy had been an unthinkable tragedy and an unbelievable miracle, that anyone could share even one of his traits was counter intuitive.

Each student was only allowed three tickets for the graduation ceremony. Cody's siblings had all wanted to come, of course, but including the in-laws (who had been part of the family longer than Cody himself), there was a grand total of six of them. So, instead of choosing one and igniting World War III, Ken had made the executive decision to give the remaining ticket to Cody's godmother instead.

After all, Raina had put a lot of effort into making sure their boy survived long enough to graduate high school. As an intensive care doctor, she had insider information on the medical community. She'd started by getting Cody set up with the best physical therapist in the area and continued giving Ken and Mary tips throughout Cody's entire recovery. Liam sometimes joked that his parents had found two new family members that night.

The lobby was packed with people, most of whom were moving. Ken had seen a video once on the internet of an intersection in Europe with something like six lanes of traffic and no stop lights. People just followed their instincts or something. The lobby reminded him of that video, only there were no lanes to make it more organized.

"Mom! Dad! Aunt Raina!" The voice was deeper than it had been when they'd first met, but still unmistakably Cody's.

The three of them turned to see him working his way towards them through the crowd. Taller than most of his classmates, Cody's head seemed to float on the mass of humanity. He grinned and waved when he caught their eyes.

Looking at him from that angle, he didn't seem any different from his classmates. Anyone asked to flip through the yearbook and pick out the kid who had suffered as he had would never have chosen correctly. It was incredible how the entire horrible event seemed to affect him so little. Physically, he still walked with a limp and had trouble manipulating the fingers on his left hand. Mentally, there were almost no visible scars.

Cody finally broke through the crowd and immediately pulled his parents into a hug. After that, he hugged Raina, too.

"We're so proud of you, honey!" Mary smiled.

"Congratulations!" Raina said.

Ken nodded at him. "Good work, kiddo."

"Thanks!" Cody grinned. "How about we get out of here? I'm starving!"

"Did you get to talk to all your friends?" Mary asked.

He shrugged. "I don't think I'll be able to find them in this crowd. Doesn't matter anyway; I'll see them at the grad parties."

"Good point," Ken said. He checked his watch. "The others should be getting to the restaurant soon. Hopefully they'll be sitting down by the time we get there so we won't have to wait."

"Yeah," Cody nodded. "I'm parked pretty close, but I can come around and get you if you want to wait here."

"I'll ride with Raina," Mary said. She squeezed Ken's bicep, smiling fondly. "Why don't you and your dad ride together?"

Ken smiled at her, then turned back to his son. "I still think you should have let me drive you."

Cody quirked an eyebrow up. "Because you haven't been in a car accident in sixty-five years?"

"No, because I'm your father." He had to reach up to tousle Cody's hair, but it was worth it. The boy still did a little dance as he tried to squirm and duck out of reach at the same time.

"Daaaad," he groaned, but he was smiling. He readjusted his graduation cap and went to hug his mom one more time before she and Raina left.

She bumped the cap with her forehead, almost knocking it off again. "Oh! I'm sorry!"

Cody just laughed and took it off completely. "No problem. It's probably not great for driving, anyway."

He asked again if Ken wanted to stay by the front door and wait for him, but the two of them ended up walking out together.

"What's the use of a brand-new knee if you can't walk out to the car?" Was Ken's argument.

He still took his cane with him sometimes. It had become superfluous after the knee replacement, and when he was in a hurry, he was known to start carrying it like a briefcase. On this day especially, he'd made sure to grab it on the way out.

Back when Cody had first come to live with them, he'd been frustrated by his limp. He'd cried into Ken's shoulder about just wanting to be normal again. The saying, "All things happen for a reason" had always been annoying, and Ken still wasn't sure he believed it, but during that time he had been grateful for his own mobility issues. It had helped him connect with Cody, let him know he wasn't alone.

After that day, the boy had started commandeering Ken's cane when he wasn't using it. At six, the cane had towered over him, looking more like a shepherd's crook or a staff. It changed Ken's own perception, transforming the object from something he was almost ashamed to have to something important. Helpful.

"I'm proud of you," he said as Cody turned out of the parking lot. "I know it was hard for you, but you got through it. You did it, kid."

"Thanks," Cody smiled, eyes darting over to him quickly before refocusing on the road.

"Cody. I know..." Ken sighed and ran a hand through his hair. "I know that what you went through back when I first found you was awful, but...I'm just so grateful you're in my life. I don't mean that I'm glad those things happened to you, it's just that, well...I'm glad you're my son."

Cody's smile stretched even further. He narrowed his eyes at the road, trying to concentrate his way out of getting emotional, but sniffed suspiciously. "Dad, I," he cleared his throat and tried again. "It wasn't fun, being in the hospital that whole time and going to physical therapy and stuff but...I think getting run over was the best thing that ever happened to me."

"What?"

"Yeah. If I hadn't, I never would have met you and Mom. So, the actual getting run over...zero out of ten stars; would not recommend. But if I had to choose, I'd definitely do it again."

Now, they were both trying to force back tears. Ken reached over and put a hand on Cody's shoulder. Even after all these years, his grip was strong, promising safety and love.

"I love you too, son."

THE UNOFFICIAL HISTORY OF THE POST-APOCALYPSE

La-a Collins and her siblings Jerome, Matice, and Sunita are no-mads. They ride horses, pulling ATV's behind them with their belongings strapped to the sides. Every morning and night, they check their horses over for any signs of illness. La-a explains that ever since the Outbreak, they've become suspicious of living things. "Most ill-nesses aren't able to pass between species," she says. After a pause, adding, "Most illnesses don't reanimate the dead, either."

La-a wears her long, gray hair in thick braids. Her mother was a hairdresser in a salon, which means she worked at a place where people would pay her to do their hair for them. She practiced on her kids, who still remember a few tricks. La-a also remembers that her mother was the one who came up with the idea for the horses in the first place. "It was kind of a joke at first," she recalls. "Back then, it felt like everyone had a plan for what they would do if there was ever a 'zombie apocalypse.' Nobody ever expected it to happen."

~ From *The History of the Apocalypse*

Daisy showed up two hours ahead of the rains, like the monsoon season had chased her from wherever she'd been before. Thunder rolled across the sky while she sat in the Common House, munching on a roll from her backpack and sipping the coffee Leeanne insisted on serving anyone who stayed at her place.

The Common House used to be a restaurant but Leeanne had converted it into a combination gathering place and hostel. Couches were spread along the walls, the center filled with folding tables. If ever there were more guests than could fit on the couches, they could easily move the tables to the storage room. Not that they'd ever have that many guests. People didn't travel much in the years after the Outbreak, and when they did they usually erred on the side of caution and kept away from strangers. Still, Leeanne was sure that hospitality was better protection against bandits than any weapon.

As one of the guys who had to actually deal with the bandits, Winter had more faith in his machete. The blade was the metal equivalent of a patchwork quilt, repaired so many times over the past three decades with whatever materials could be scavenged that it had as many tones and hues as the forest. He rewrapped the handle every couple years, but within a month each new hilt had the imprint of his hand pressed into it. He kept it with him at all times.

When he sauntered into the common house, it was the first part of him that caught Daisy's attention. She'd glanced up at the sound of the bell, which warned whenever someone entered or exited the house. She didn't even look at Winter himself, eyes magnetically drawn to the weapon. As she stared, a clicking sound came from the battered silver laptop that rested on her knees. Winter couldn't see the keyboard, but he could tell by the way the muscles in her bare forearms flexed that she was typing something.

She didn't bother looking at the man himself until he crouched in front of her, deliberately hiding the blade from view. Her fingers slowed, and she dragged her eyes to his face. It was one of those faces that looked haunted despite its youth, which was fairly normal in those days. Deep brown eyes bored into her, hard with purpose, but his chestnut hair was touseled boyishly.

She smiled. "Hi. I'm Daisy Johansen."

"That your bike out front?" Winter asked.

She preened. "It is. Isn't she a beauty?"

He ignored her question. "What brings you to the valley?"

"It was on my way," she shrugged one shoulder. "Do you have names here?"

"Of course."

Daisy raised her eyebrows and waited.

Weathered moccasins embroidered with sun motifs stepped up to them. A hand that had darkened during the summer from almond to a shade just lighter than her coffee held out a steaming mug to Winter. He took it automatically.

"Need a refill, traveler?" Leeanne asked, smiling.

Daisy smiled back. "As long as you have the beans for it."

Leeanne laughed. "No need to worry about that. And don't let Winter bother you, either. He's harmless as long as you don't try to eat anyone."

Winter glowered up at her and she kicked him lightly in the shin. She was older than his mother, but seemed to have a gene that stopped her from hardening with experience like the other adults. The only lines on her face were from laughing.

You can tell a lot about a person from the lines on their face. Like winds, once you see which direction they're most likely to come from, you can usually figure out what they're going to be like. That was why Winter never trusted younger people – *especially* people his own age, who were old enough to do damage but too young to truly understand the consequences. Daisy was around his age, maybe even a little younger. Her face was smeared with dust and sweat that she'd tried to wipe off, but underneath the grime was skin smooth as milk. Even worse, her eyes reminded him of a fox; calculating and cataloging everything.

"So, Winter," Daisy said. "Are you the welcoming committee, or do you just like sharing drinks with strange women?"

"I'm one of the guardians of this town," he said. "I keep an eye on the Common House and other buildings in the center. I *investigate* strange women – or men – who show up uninvited."

"Interesting." Daisy's fingers started up again. "I saw a sign on my way in that said 'Harvest Valley'. Is that the name of this place?"

"Have you gotten looked over by the doctor yet?" He countered.

Daisy's smile slipped. "Oh…sorry, I didn't see a sign coming in—"

"Unless this is your first time away from home, you should know this by now."

"Look, I'm sorry. I'll go right now, okay?" Daisy hit a few buttons and folded up her computer, stuffing it in an old backpack.

Winter stood up with her. "I'll go with you."

"It's a date." She had to look up to hold his gaze, but she wasn't backing down. An afterthought interrupted her determined glare, and she turned back to Leeanne. Daisy held her mug out, but Leeanne waved her off.

"Finish your coffee, hon. You can return the mug when you come back tonight."

Daisy nodded. She turned to Winter and swept her arm grandly as if she were a queen telling him to lead the way. His frown deepened. He marched to the door and held it open for her, bowing deeply. She made a sound that might have been a laugh if she hadn't strangled it.

The two of them stepped out into the gathering darkness. It wasn't even noon, but the heavy clouds had almost completely blocked out the sun. Daisy's motorcycle was chained to a rusted bench, bags slung across the seat and a plate of interlocking obsidian slats spread across the handlebars. Catching his look, Daisy gestured to it. Another clap of thunder drowned out what she tried to say. Winter could see her mouth moving, but all he could hear was the coming storm.

"What?" He asked when the sky had quieted down.

"I said they're solar panels," she said. "They convert sunlight into electricity. My mom hooked them up."

"Don't think you're likely to get much sun in the next few weeks."

She made a face and started folding the plates up. When she was finished, she pulled up the seat to reveal a long, narrow compartment stretching up to the handlebars. Daisy tucked the solar panels inside, then grabbed a tarp from a saddlebag and draped it over the whole machine, securing it with bungee cord.

Winter watched, barely able to contain his impatience. Finally, he turned and started leading her further into the city.

"How long has this town been around?" She glanced at the buildings they walked past. "It's clear it's not new, but is it pre-Midas?"

"How should I know?" Winter asked, annoyed.

"Don't you have an origin story or something? Local lore?"

"No."

Daisy raised an eyebrow and he sighed.

"All I know is that my parents and the other survivors in the area grouped up about thirty years ago. I don't know if they lived here before or found the place abandoned and set up camp."

"Is there someone who *would* know? Are your parents still around?"

"I'm not going to take you sight-seeing before I find out if you've got Midas," Winter snapped.

Daisy held her hands up. "Sor-ry."

The Midas virus was named after the story of the king who got exactly what he wished for only to watch it ruin his life in the end. In the story, all King Midas had to do was touch something (or someone), and it would turn to solid gold. "That was a convenient detail," says Phineas Garmin, "because the Midas virus can be passed by direct contact. Of course, the contact has to be somewhere there's a route to the inside of the person, like the mouth or an open wound." Phineas is a doctor from Nestle, North America. He remembers watching the News with his father during the first stages of the apocalypse.

No one knows anymore exactly how it started. Some claim it was a freak mutation of some other virus. Some are convinced it was a miracle cure gone wrong. It started out with flulike symptoms that got worse and worse until the victim eventually died. "That's where the Midas part comes in," explains Phineas. "At first, you seemed to get exactly what you wanted: after twelve hours, the victim would come back to life. But it wasn't really the victim anymore; just a body, reanimated and feral. And, worst of all, contagious."

~ From *The History of the Apocalypse*

For a moment, they walked in silence. Leeanne's Common House was pretty far from the town line. The hospital – such as it was -- being the first building anyone would pass. Winter's mother had been the one to make sure of that. She'd designed the wall so there was only one way in. Winter ground his teeth thinking about how Daisy had to have gone *right past* the building with the word "HOSPITAL" painted in ten-foot-tall letters on the side. He sucked in a breath and let it out again. If he killed her, she'd probably drop the mug in the struggle. He didn't want to see the heartbroken look on Leeanne's face if he brought back the shards.

"What's it matter, anyway?" He surprised himself by asking.

She crossed her arms over her chest and lifted her chin. "History is important. We have to tell our stories so our descendants know where they came from."

"Why would they need to know about the past?" Winter scoffed. "They're not living there. Or, here, I guess."

"For one thing, if you know that doing something didn't work out well before, you're less likely to try it yourself," she said. "Like, I don't know…trying to cure death?"

Fantastic, Winter thought. *She's a conspiracy theorist.* Fortunately, they'd reached the hospital doors. Winter shoved through them and strode up to the desk.

The doctor was sitting on a metal folding chair behind the desk. One hand was running compulsively through his red hair, gripping sections and releasing them at random. He didn't even look up when the door banged shut behind Daisy; he was completely lost in the paperback he held in the other hand. The pages were yellow and wrinkled, which made sense. Winter was pretty sure the doctor had read that particular book at least twenty times.

It was a thin book, small enough to fit into a back pocket. There was no real cover or spine, just printed pages sewn together on one side. The kind of book made post-apocalypse by people who found printers or scanners that both still worked *and* had ink. Books like that were distributed sporadically, printed whenever possible by whoever had the means and motivation. The old world had produced much nicer looking books, but there was something about the new ones that encouraged people to pay traveling merchants top dollar. Maybe it was just so they could have tangible proof that the world was still spinning – that life went on.

"Franklin," Winter called, projecting his voice loud enough to reach the doctor in whatever corner of his brain he was curled up in.

Franklin lifted his head and blinked slowly as if waking from a trance. He opened his mouth to ask what was wrong, then caught sight of Daisy. Question answered, he flipped the book upside down on the desk and stood. He raised an eyebrow at Winter.

"Are you going to introduce me?" He asked. His voice was perpetually rough and dry, thanks to a patient a few years back who had tested Midas-positive. Franklin had gone to sedate the patient and gotten clocked in the throat. Thanks to Winter, who had accompanied them, he'd escaped with only a broken wind-pipe.

"This is Daisy," Winter said. "She just got in, needs a test."

"Makes sense." Franklin smiled and gestured to a room off to the side. "If you'll just step into my office, we can get you on your way in about half an hour."

Winter trailed behind them, one hand resting on the hilt of his blade.

"In school it was always, 'when are we going to use this in real life?', you know? We were convinced they weren't teaching us anything relevant," Jenny Tucker says. She's twenty-three, with blonde hair and a scar running from the underside of her jaw across her neck. "The Outbreak hit when I was a junior in high school. I never thought expected to get so much use out of my biology textbook."

She shows me a thick, battered book. The hardcover is chipped and faded, the pages wrinkled with use and water damage. Bookmarks are scattered throughout, allowing her quick access to the most important sections. Her favorites are the chapters on the skeletal and muscular structures of the human body. There are tons of notes scribbled in the margins.

"I've even dissected a few zombies," she boasts, using the colloquial term. "If things ever go back to normal, I might become a surgeon."

~ From The History of the Apocalypse

"I hate to say I told you so," Daisy said, stretching her arms over her head. "But I told you so."

"If you hate it, stop smiling," Winter suggested.

"I don't hate it that much." She leaned towards the edge of the area protected by the building's awning as if she was going to peek up at the sky to see how much more rain was up there.

The heavy rain pelted the earth like a bunch of angels had tipped over a bucket from the sky. Winter knew better than to think of it in those terms. Buckets could only hold a finite amount of water. The monsoon season was a time when water was spontaneously generated in the clouds, immediately replacing anything they lost. Even the breaks between storms were full of invisible water, hanging heavy and wet in the air and blanketing people with phantom quilts they couldn't squirm out of.

"I needed a shower anyway," Daisy murmured.

Winter sighed and pointed across the street. It was blurred by the rain, like a heat mirage. "Most of the buildings have overhangs. If we move quickly, we should be able to get back to the Common House without drowning."

Daisy pursed her lips and nodded.

"Okay," Winter readied himself. "On my mark."

"Wait!" Daisy knelt down, swinging her backpack onto the sidewalk beside her.

She pulled out her laptop and leaned it against the side of the hospital while she hunted through the rest of the pack. Finally, she tugged out a roll of purple, slick, shiny fabric with a rubber band around it. It made a squeaky sound when it brushed against literally anything. She pulled off the rubber band, sticking it on her wrist while she unrolled it.

It was a cheap poncho, about three or four times too big for her. Winter was used to seeing people with clothes that weren't necessarily their size; everyone made do with what they could. It was just a little strange that Daisy would be carrying something around that she hadn't altered to fit her. Especially seeing as she was some sort of nomad.

She wrapped her laptop up in the poncho and shoved both back inside her bag. Well. That explained that. Straightening up, she swung it back over her shoulders and nodded to Winter.

"Okay. Ready."

He looked up and down the street a few times. The downpour was loud enough to drown out any cars or carts coming at them, and he didn't want to get squashed.

"On three?" He suggested.

"Sure."

"One…" He looked both ways again. "Two…" He bent his legs, preparing himself to get drenched. He looked around one last time. "Three!"

Winter and Daisy sprinted across the street, muscles straining. It felt like they were trying to break through an actual, physical wall. Was there even any space between the raindrops? As Winter forged ahead, he felt like he'd been cut off from the rest of the world. There was nothing but the water pounding down on him, running over him, crashing under his feet. He couldn't hear his steps or see far enough ahead to be sure he was even moving. He just had to push aside his feelings and trust that his body was doing what it needed to keep him alive.

They burst through the other side. Without the resistance of the rain, Winter surged forward and almost collided with the brick wall of the mechanic's shop. Next to him, Daisy was laughing like a little girl.

Oh, she survived, Winter observed. He didn't know if he was disappointed about that or not.

"That…" Daisy had one arm braced against the building, but she flung the other out to point at the storm. "Was amazing."

Winter rolled his eyes. "You've never been caught in the rain before?"

"*That* wasn't getting 'caught in the rain,'" she made air quotes with her fingers. "*That* was swimming through a spontaneously occurring river."

"Not everything has to be poetic," he said. His clothes were half soaked. He checked his watch and debated changing before the end of his shift.

"Not everything has to be boring," she retorted. And then she honest-to-goodness *stuck her tongue out at him.*

He had three hours left. He could wait. "Well, now that I know you're clean, why don't you go back for that coffee? I'm sure Leeanne will be happy to see you."

"Now that you know I'm clean," she twisted to pull a small metal box out of her back pocket. She flipped the clasp and the top popped off to reveal a tiny notebook and even tinier pencil. "Would you mind answering a few questions?"

"Yeah. I do mind." Winter turned away and tossed a wave over his shoulder. "Enjoy your stay." He'd usually go the other direction on his patrol, but his usual path went right by Leeanne's Common House and he did not want to spend more time with the woman-child than he had to.

Daisy crossed her arms and huffed at his back, but she was smiling. One of the things she loved about traveling was meeting all the different people. For example, this punk who couldn't be much older than her, strutting around like the OG Tough Guy so people would Take Him Seriously™. She scribbled a quick description of him on the first clean page of her notebook, then shut the box and slid it back into her pocket.

She strolled when she was protected by the overhangs – well, mostly protected. Rain did bounce off the street and spray up at her even when she was underneath them. That was how she got back to the Common House; a few yards of strolling followed by intense sprinting under torrential rain. By the time she pushed open Leeanne's door, she was pretty sure her body was ninety-five percent water.

Daisy resisted the urge to shake herself like a dog. It was rude. Also, the sonic waves the place was generating had a good chance of blowing the water off her.

Five men were on stage, their microphones and instruments plugged into a small generator, but they were only responsible for maybe half the noise. The voices of the people crowded into the Common House flowed into all the cracks left by the music like water around rocks until the whole building was full to bursting with sound.

Daisy looked around, suddenly unsure this was the place she'd come from a little over an hour earlier. The tables and chairs were in the same places, but instead of a quiet crowd sipping coffee and munching on biscuits, this crowd was drinking golden liquid from tall glasses. The rain outside shook the care from their volume. It twisted and blossomed like a wild rosebush. This was life in a different filter than it had been earlier. Even Leeanne had changed into more brightly colored clothes.

Daisy's eyes slowly adjusted to the brightness of the crowd. There was hardly any place left to sit. Besides two open stools at the bar, the only open places were at tables that already had people sitting at them. That was perfect. She wanted to sit with other people, but if there'd been more open space, inserting herself into a group might come off as creepy. The guys onstage ended their song and everyone applauded. Daisy cupped her hands to make her claps a little louder and sauntered over to the nearest table. Three of the five chairs were already taken by kids probably even younger than her. Excellent. People who didn't have the pre-apocalyptic world clouding their judgement were the best sources for her book.

"Can I sit with you guys?" She asked.

The trio looked up at her. The girl and the taller of the two boys had sunset-colored hair and identical brown eyes. He smiled; she didn't. The other boy, with chestnut-brown skin and long black hair tied in a braid, quirked up half his mouth in a compromise.

"Go ahead," the redheaded boy gestured to the open seat.

"Thanks." Daisy grinned and sat next to him with a squelch. She grimaced and they all laughed. Even the girl.

The band onstage struck up a new song. Four out of five members played some sort of stringed instrument – one was definitely a guitar, the others looked like various sizes of violin. The fifth member sat behind a drum set painted neon green with "The Afterthought" scrawled across the head of the bass.

"Did someone steal your umbrella?" The girl asked, smirking.

"Ah," Daisy shrugged and cast her mind back. "I think I left it somewhere east of the Mississippi."

"Most people just say 'Mississippi'," the girl commented.

"I think she meant the river," the ebony-haired boy corrected.

"Oh." The girl rubbed the back of her neck and they all laughed again.

"I'm Cole," the redheaded boy said. "This is my sister, Rhea, and that's Ishkode."

Ishkode flipped her a peace sign.

"I'm Daisy," she said.

"You from the river?" Rhea asked.

Daisy shrugged. "I don't actually know. I've been traveling around for as long as I can remember. I assume I'm from this continent, but that's about it."

"Really?" Cole leaned forward, eyes sparkling. "I've always wanted to travel! Aren't you worried about Midas?"

"Yeah, did you get checked out by Doc?" Rhea narrowed her eyes. "You've had your shots, right?"

Daisy held up her left arm, even though the needle mark was no longer visible. "Just got my latest booster two weeks ago. Actually, the reason I got caught in the rain was because Franklin was checking me out."

Name-dropping the doctor was apparently the right thing to do, because Rhea's shoulders relaxed a few inches. Ishkode pulled his chair in a little so a tall woman in a flowing skirt could get past. A dog the color of a toasted marshmallow followed at her heels, and suddenly the bare concrete floor made so much more sense.

"Is it just you traveling around?" he asked, taking advantage of the reduced distance between them.

The question nailed her in the chest, but she shook it off. "When I was younger, I used to travel with my mom. Now it's just me."

They all nodded in the way people nod when they want to ask more questions but are too polite to press. The guitar player hit a series of chords in rapid succession to wrap up the song. The audience clapped again.

"Thank you!" The lead singer, who was playing an instrument almost as tall as he was, said as he leaned into the microphone. "This next one is going to be a singalong, so sing along if you know the words." He counted off to his band, then showcased his vocal range. "*Whee-EEE-eee-eee, whee-um-bum-buh-way...*"

"I can't imagine that," Rhea said. "Don't you ever want to just find somewhere to stay? A home?"

"Actually," Daisy tried hard not to grin at the perfect opening. "I have to travel. I'm writing a book."

"Really?" Ishkode's eyebrows shot up and he leaned forward again, sans dog this time. "What about? Geography?"

"History," she said. "I'm calling it *The Unofficial History of the Post-Apocalypse.*"

"What's it about; the way towns got established or something?" Rhea wondered.

"It's about what people are doing now." Daisy knew her eyes were bright, and she hoped they wouldn't scare the trio off. "There are millions of history books that were written about what happened before Midas, at least one that was written about Midas, but there need to be books written about right now, too."

"Is there actually anything interesting happening now, though? Like; people are just living their lives. Zombie attacks hardly ever happen anymore, and when they do we're prepared for them and they're not a big deal. Do you really think anyone will want to read about boring, everyday stuff?"

"But to them it might not *be* boring, everyday stuff! It's boring to us, because we're living it, but what about people who never experience life like we have?"

"That's a good point," Ishkode said. "I mean, my parents have a bunch of books about how our ancestors lived before Europeans even got here and all that stuff was probably boring and normal to them at the time, but now it's precious to us because it's a link to where we came from."

"Exactly!" Daisy pointed at him, grinning. "That's what I'm hoping my book will be someday."

"Cool." He nodded, respect blooming in his eyes. They were brown, but when he flicked them down to meet her gaze, they caught the light and shifted into molten gold.

"Do you want to interview *us*?" Cole asked eagerly.

"If you don't mind," Daisy replied, digging her metal-encased notebook out of her back pocket.

"Awesome!"

She opened the notebook and flipped to an open page. "So, did you all grow up here?"

The first few months after the Midas outbreak, the majority of the population did their best to continue living life as they always had. A national organization called the Center for Disease Control – colloquially; the CDC – did their best to find ways to maintain the status quo. Eventually, even they were forced to change their recommendation from wearing masks and social distancing to sheltering in place. Still, some people – and employers – persisted.

Were those proud few valiantly loyal or simply too stubborn to see what was happening? Both. Neither. Truly, there's no real answer.

Sometimes, it's too hard to adjust to something new after being raised to believe that the world works in a certain way. Other times, there are nations, people, or causes that stand for something people are willing to support to the very end...or die trying.

~ The History of the Apocalypse

Winter shook off his umbrella as best he could under the Common House's overhang before coming inside. It was lucky he'd been heading with the wind instead of against it, or the umbrella would've been mutilated beyond repair. The bell announced his presence, and a few patrons groaned. Their clothes were rumpled and their hair slightly mussed. He smirked and wondered if they'd spent the night. A few of the more rested-looking attempted to hide their own amusement behind conveniently timed sips of coffee.

Winter scanned the room. His quarry was still sleeping, curled up on one of the couches with her bomber jacket spread over her, head resting on her backpack. A pencil was stuck behind her ear – how it had stayed there all night was a mystery. She was still in the clothes she'd worn when she arrived.

Leeanne intercepted him on the way over, offering him a steaming mug.

"Thanks," he said. He blew on the surface of the beautiful black liquid and took a sip. "How did it go last night?"

"About average for a normal Wednesday," she said. "Impressive for a stormy Wednesday, though."

"Glad to hear it." He squinted at Daisy, trying to decide if she was actually sleeping or just trying to avoid him. "Did you have any trouble with Lois Lane over there?"

Leeanne shook her head. "Everyone seemed to enjoy having her."

"*Everyone*?" He raised an eyebrow. "What, did she join the band or something?"

"I think she talked to everyone in the place." Leeanne shook her head, smiling. "She might be even more fond of company than I am."

"She was interviewing people last night?" Winter frowned. "She sure doesn't waste any time."

Daisy shifted, forehead creasing before she let out a small sigh.

"You don't think she's planning on heading out before the storm has passed, do you?"

Leeanne raised an eyebrow at him. "Why do you ask? Has she grown on you already?"

Winter chugged the last of his coffee. It was still hot and practically melted the flesh from his throat on the way down, but Leeanne had her mischief-making face on and he needed to take evasive actions immediately. He pushed the mug into her hands and saluted.

"Thanks for the coffee. I'll see you around."

As he turned, he saw Daisy stretch and open her eyes. Of course, she'd wake up right when he was leaving. His steps faltered, but he forced himself towards the door. Sticking around to talk to her would just encourage Leeanne. He'd have to come up with a way to randomly bump into her later. Not because he was interested in her personally, but because he was a guardian. It was his job to make sure people didn't go riding off into thunderstorms just to hydroplane, spin off the road, and die five miles out of town. Bodies attracted scavengers like wild animals. And zombies.

He was still trying to come up with a plan a few hours later, when he actually did run into her by accident. The guardians were scouring the town to see if anyone needed help after that first day of heavy rain. It had let up a bit; it was a downpour instead of an attempt to create a liquid atmosphere. Winter was checking in with the Mall Rats when he found her.

The "Mall Rats" were the scavengers who took over what used to be a strip mall in the center of town. Their place of business – and, for some of them, residence – was the "Mall" part. The "Rat" part was a reference to how they got their inventory. Once a month, the Mall Rats would close up shop for a week or two and drive around the area exploring the wreckage in search of things they could sell. Digging around in trash or ruins created a high risk of infection. The townsfolk avoided them like plague-bearing rodents, only getting within arms-length to shop.

Honestly, he should have expected to find Daisy with them.

At first, when Winter entered the first store, he thought he'd interrupted a meeting. Usually, the Rats spread out along the different stores, organizing and reorganizing their merchandise. Unless they were doing some construction, there were usually only one to three Rats per storefront at any given time. When he opened the door, at least twenty pairs of eyes snapped to him.

Daisy was sitting on an armchair made of faded leather and gaping tears, only half of which had been mended. She was writing furiously. The alpha Rat, Jennika, was perched on a shiny black barstool only a few feet away from her. The place was practically infested. Winter recognized most of the business managers and a good seventy-five percent of the rest. They were crowded around

Daisy like she was a fully functioning espresso machine complete with grounds and fresh milk.

Jennika was in the middle of a story, gesticulating wildly. Her tattoo sleeves were fully visible with her tank top on. Winter noticed that she'd followed through on her plan to paint her prosthetic to match her flesh arm. A few years before, she'd cut her right hand during one of the scavenging trips. It had gotten infected, and they were too far from a doctor to find out if it was Midas or not. So, she downed half a bottle of whiskey and her friends cut her arm off below the elbow, then cauterized the wound.

"Brrr." Daisy shivered, smirking. "Anyone else cold? It's getting a little Wintery in here."

Laughter broke behind her like a wave against a rock, spraying sound everywhere.

"Hilarious." Winter put a hand on his hip and looked around. "Everything alright here? No problems with the weather so far?"

"How considerate," Jennika drawled. She twisted around in her chair to cast a look around the room. "We did do a check today, right?"

"Course we did!" A tall, blue-haired Rat made a face and crossed his arms. "It's the first day of Monsoon Season."

"Right, which is why the guardians are checking around with everyone," Winter said.

He felt out of place, standing about six inches from the door. Daisy was on her chair backwards, arms folded on the back. As she watched the exchange, she rested her head on them. It put her face dangerously close to Jennika. The alpha Rat wouldn't even have to move if she wanted to ruffle the writer's hair. Winter's free hand twitched with the instinctive urge to pull her away before she was contaminated.

If he thought about it, though, there was probably a higher chance of *Daisy* being infectious than any of the Rats. They'd been back in town for weeks; she'd just showed up the day before. If she belonged anywhere in town, it was with the Mall Rats.

"Okay. Good. Let someone know if you need help." Winter pivoted and headed out the door.

Outside, he shoved his hands in his pockets and stared into the rain. The wind was blowing so hard it looked like it was coming down sideways. He'd had a plan, some sort of strategy for getting around his section of town so he stayed as dry as possible. For some reason, he was completely blanking on it. Tilting his head up, he searched his memory. Maybe the problem was that he'd planned to check the mall shops one by one. Or maybe the fact that he'd run into Daisy in the middle of his rounds instead of after was throwing him off.

The door opened behind him and someone ran into his back. He stumbled off the edge of the sidewalk into the rain. Cold water dumped on his head, running down his neck and rebooting his brain.

"I'm sorry!" Daisy said. Her voice was sincere, but she was biting her lip to keep from laughing.

He glowered back at her, stomping back to the shelter of the overhang. "What are you doing?"

She was the persona version of a quick-change artist. Suddenly professional, she said, "I came to interview you."

"Oh. Uh...no." He dipped his head and stared pointedly at her. "Thanks for asking."

"Right, sorry. *Can* I interview you?"

"Still no." Winter turned on his heel and darted across the street to the next overhang.

"Hey--!" Heavy splashing indicated Daisy wasn't about to give up that easily.

Winter sighed and kept walking. If he just ignored her, maybe she would go away. The building he was in front of at the moment was abandoned. The adjoining building was also officially abandoned, but everybody knew there was a group of kids living in the apartment upstairs. He pushed the door open and stepped inside the forest of dust that used to be a beauty parlor. The door didn't swing shut right away because someone wasn't taking a hint.

A few posters survived on the walls above counters covered in literal inches of dust. They were faded and peeling. It was impossible to tell what most of them had been, but one or two had vague silhouettes like nuclear shadows. Deep sinks where patrons used to have their hair washed were just baskets of dust and mold.

"Where are you going?" Daisy coughed. "Nobody's been in this place for decades."

"You sure about that?" Despite himself, Winter pointed at the floor. Years of footprints had worn a strip along the linoleum that looked absolutely spotless compared to every other surface.

Daisy gasped, eyes widening. She dug into her back pocket for her notebook.

Winter didn't wait for her, heading along the path to a side door. The cramped hallway behind it probably used to be the break room, judging by the gutted computer and the wreck of what had once been a spinning chair. Just to his left was a staircase. It was dark, and he ran one hand along the railing just in case.

Footsteps pounded up behind him, but he didn't turn around. There was a small landing in front of the door to the second floor. Winter knocked loudly, then stuck his hands back in his pockets and waited.

He tossed a look over his shoulder. "We don't officially know these kids are here, okay? Don't spook them."

"Sure thing." Daisy nodded.

Usually it took a few minutes of knocking and waiting for someone to show up, but in the past couple years the kids had begun to expect the annual check-ins. The door opened just enough for a tall boy to slip out into the hall. He carried a lantern that bounced light along the walls and illuminated bits and pieces of the three of them. He was thin, but his face was still rounded with baby fat. Dark almond eyes seemed to want to hide beneath inky bangs as much as their owner wanted to hide back in the apartment. But they narrowed as if in a challenge.

"Hey, Leo," Winter said. "Everything okay in here?"

"Off the record," Daisy added.

Leo's eyes flicked to her for a minute, then returned to Winter. "Everything's fine."

"Do you know what 'off the record' means?" Daisy asked.

"No." Leo's voice was quiet and short, like he was trying not to be noticed.

"It means nothing you say can be legally repeated," she explained. "So, you can tell us anything and we won't be able to tell anyone else."

He frowned, searching Winter's face. Winter had never heard about 'off the record' before, but he nodded like it was standard practice. Leo relaxed just the tiniest bit.

"Some tree branches came through one of the windows," he said. "But we got them out and boarded it up."

"Did anyone get cut on the glass?" Winter asked.

Leo moved his free hand behind his leg. When he saw Winter's pointed look, he sighed and held it out. "It's nothing. Just a couple cuts. I didn't even notice right away."

Winter took out his pocket flashlight and pointed it at the hand. Whoever had bandaged it had done a good job. The cloth wrapped around it looked clean. The palm of Leo's hand was snugly mummified, but none of his fingers were purple so it wasn't too tight. The blood hadn't seeped through, either, which was always a good sign.

"Make sure you rebandage this every day. Keep the wounds clean. And if you see *any* sign of infection, you go to Franklin." Winter shone his flashlight directly into Leo's eyes. "Clear?"

Leo squinted against the light, mouth twisting up in a smirk. "Yeah. Clear."

"Good." Winter put his flashlight away and paused. "If you're worried about it, tell Franklin the whole thing is *off the record,* okay?"

The lantern bobbed along with Leo's nod. "I will."

"Alright. Stay safe." Winter turned to head back out. Daisy wiggled her fingers in a wave, then scrambled down the stairs so he didn't run her over.

"That was pretty cool," she said.

They were outside and she was still following him.

"Is that 'off the record' thing real, or did you just make it up?" He asked.

She grinned like he'd stepped into her trap. "It's real! People used to use it all the time in the pre-Midas days. History can be pretty interesting, you know."

Winter rolled his eyes and jumped between two overhangs. The next three buildings were empty, and then they'd be at the tailor shop. Maybe he could lose her there. Except…ditching her didn't seem as important as it had earlier.

"I still don't understand why anyone would want to read about what's happening right now," he said.

"People want to know how other people live," Daisy told him. "They want to know how similar they are, and how different. We all have a little anthropologist in us."

"I don't even want to know what that means."

"The study of humans."

"Why don't they just say that?"

"Well, to answer that I'll have to tell you a little history."

"Pass." Winter looked at her. "Oh, I was actually going to look for you later."

She smirked. "Could've fooled me."

"Yeah, well," he waved a hand. "It's not later yet. Anyway, I wanted to make sure you're not thinking about heading out in this mess."

"You don't strike me as the kind of guy who gets attached easily. What gives?"

"I'm not *attached*. It's my job to make sure people don't do stupid stuff." He shoved his hands in his pockets and picked up the pace. Daisy had to almost jog to keep up with him.

"Yeah…" She tripped over the curb, rain dumping on her head as soon as she left the shelter of the overhang. She jogged to catch up to Winter on the other side. "Hey, can we talk sometime? I'm interested in what you guardians do."

"No."

"Why not?"

He pulled open a glass door covered in plywood. A cool breeze blew out, ruffling their clothes. "Because it's boring. It'll be a waste of time for both of us. Trust me."

"Hey! Shut the door! You're letting all the cool out!" called Stacy McGregor from inside.

The two of them hurried in and shut the door behind them. Stacy had four fans going, one in each corner of the room. Fabric and thread were safe in drawers – they could see them through the clear plastic. The woman herself was settled near the back wall with her sewing machine.

Besides the millions of drawers and cabinets, there were a few racks of clothes and two wardrobes. The clothes on the racks swayed back and forth in the breeze from the fans. Little tags hung from them, fluttering like trapped moths. Most of Stacy's business came from altering clothes people brought in, but in her spare time she designed and created clothes. If a design turned out particularly well, she would keep it for herself.

"Hi, Stace. Just checking in," Winter said.

"How nice of you." She kept her hands where they were, holding the fabric carefully in place, but she let the machine slow down and turned to face them. "Who's this? You're a little young to have an apprentice."

"This is—"

"Daisy Johansen," she interrupted. "I'm a writer." Stepping forward, she held out her hand. Stacy raised an eyebrow and Daisy dropped her hand, blushing. "Sorry."

"What's a writer doing following a guardian around?"

Daisy put her hands on her hips and rolled her eyes. "I was *trying* to get him to talk to me, but he's being stubborn."

Stacy laughed. "Why do you need to talk to a guardian? Is it a mystery story?"

"Actually, it's about what people have been doing since the Midas virus breakout."

"Really?" Stacy raised an eyebrow.

Daisy's eyes lit up like a fox spotting a wounded rabbit. She got her notebook out. "You know, I'd love to interview *you*, if you don't mind."

Stacy straightened, pleased. "Why not?" She did her best to gesture with an elbow. "Find a seat anywhere."

"So..." Winter shifted. "I'm guessing you're good here?"

"Yeah. Thanks." Stacy tossed her head in his direction in what might have been a nod of acknowledgment.

"Okay then." Winter waited a minute, but both of them seemed to forget he was there. *That's a good thing,* he reminded himself as he left.

Ironically, there are times when trying to evacuate a city actually makes the situation worse. Traffic jams are buffets for Midas hordes because their victims can't get away. Some people ditch their cars and run for it, which only works in the short term. Let's face it; if the survivors were prepared to go on foot, they'd be going on foot.

Getting out and running means leaving behind some if not all tools and supplies.

Over the thousands of years humans have built "civilizations", our status as apex predators has gotten less attention. Another twisted irony is how Midas reminded us of that fact. Humans are pursuit predators, which means we don't run after our prey; we track and follow slowly. Of all the aspects of humanity Midas strips from its victims, this part is left alone. If you ever find yourself running from a Midas horde, don't let your guard down because you think you've gotten far enough ahead. Slow and steady still wins the race.

~ from *The History of the Apocalypse*

The hospital officially opened at seven in the morning. Winter showed up at seven fifteen. Franklin barely looked up when the door opened. He was reading that book again, hunched over his desk and staring at the pages like they held the secrets of the universe.

"Are you busy?" Winter asked, crossing his arms.

Franklin looked up, then back at his book, then up again as if he wasn't sure. "I mean, is it an emergency?"

Winter shrugged. "I just wanted to see how Daisy's cultures have turned out."

"Mm-hm…" Franklin sighed heavily and put his book down. Getting up, he stretched his arms over his head until something popped. "Come on, I'll show you."

They headed back into his lab. It was a closet-sized space off to the right of the room he saw most patients in. When his predecessor had been in charge, the lab had been lit only by a bare bulb in the ceiling. Franklin had gotten some lamps from the Mall

Rats and set them up in strategic locations so he could, as he said, "actually see what I'm doing."

Their local tech wizard, Rochelle, had Frankenstein'd whatever machines he'd found so they actually worked. He could run analyses on nearly everything. Not that Winter could put a name to any of them. He was pretty sure one was half-toaster, but that was the best he could do.

In the middle of the room was a giant computer tower. Or, at least, it *looked* giant compared to the monitor. The tower was made even higher by the box on top of it which housed several terabyte drives. It wasn't just books Franklin refused to get rid of; he had every test result he'd ever gotten saved up. Just in case. The one he was in the process of filling was hooked up to the tower itself, and it would stay connected until there wasn't a byte of space left on it.

Franklin thumbed a button on the tower and yawned as it booted up. The screen flickered and buzzed as it booted up. Winter crossed his arms tighter and looked at the other machines, muscles tense.

"Hey, Frank, none of these things are contagious, right?"

Franklin half-turned and followed his gaze. "Not unless you drink them," he smirked.

"You're sure?" Winter glared at a centrifuge like it had insulted him. "Aren't there like...I don't know, air parts or something?"

Franklin rolled his eyes. "Airborne particles? You're safe. Relax." He leaned over to type his login into the bar that appeared on the screen. "Or, you know, wait outside."

"I'm fine."

"Okay then." He shrugged.

His desktop was clogged with folders marked with random-looking mixes of letters and numbers. Franklin opened one and pulled up a document. It was in medical-ese, so all Winter really understood was Daisy's name at the top.

"Translation?" He requested.

"She's clean," Franklin said. "No trace of Midas."

Winter let out a relieved breath. "Good, because I think she's interviewed half the town by now."

Franklin laughed. "She's definitely her mother's daughter."

"You know her mom?"

Franklin gave Winter his full attention for the first time that day, eyebrows raised in disbelief. "Are you serious?"

"*Yes.*" The longer Winter stayed here, the dumber he felt.

Franklin shook his head and got up, leading him back to the lobby. He picked up the book he was always reading and handed it over. Winter turned it over in his hands. The cover page was simple; strong black lettering on normal paper. The ink had faded over time to a smoky blue, but it was still legible.

"Oh wow," he murmured.

It's a little like someone hit the rewind button on the society. Pre-Midas, North America was mostly industrial. Farms were disappearing. Now that Midas has broken out, people are fleeing to the country and trying their hands at self-sufficiency. The biggest problem with that is most people don't know how to farm. It's a bit frightening, the damage you can do when you don't know what you're doing.

~ The History of the Apocalypse, Violet Johansen

Sometimes, you're not aware of a noise until it's gone. When Winter stepped outside, it took him a minute to pinpoint exactly what was strange. Then he realized the rain had stopped. There were holes in the clouds, patches of sunlight peeking through and landing on the ground like reverse shadows. It felt like a weight had lifted. He looked up and down the street instinctively before crossing, which is when he noticed Daisy. She was perched on top of the town wall, typing on her computer. Sunlight reflected with blinding intensity off what looked like a mat next to her. He guessed it was one of her solar power collection things.

Winter hadn't climbed the wall since he was a teenager, but he still knew all the shortcuts and handholds on the way up. They came to him as he climbed, floating up through years of more recent memories.

The wall was a good three feet thick, so Daisy was able to sit cross-legged the way she liked. Winter hauled himself up next to her and swung his legs over the outside. He looked out at the empty space that stretched out for a mile on every side of the town. With all the heavy rain they were getting, they'd have to get the gardeners to clear it out soon. They needed to be able to see if something was coming.

He glanced at her. Like the first day they'd met, Daisy watched him without pausing in her typing.

"How do you do that?" He asked.

She smiled. "You just memorize the keys, and after a while it's automatic."

"Huh. Cool." He looked away again. "Can I ask you something?"

"Your politeness is scaring me," she teased. "Yeah, go ahead."

He took a deep breath. "Why is your book called *The* Unofficial *History of the Post-Apocalypse* if your mom wrote the first one?"

She stopped typing. After a beat of silence, she closed the laptop and set it down beside her, scooting forward to drop her legs off the side. This time, she was the one who looked away.

"Mom was working on a sequel," she began. "It was going to be called *The History of the Post-Apocalypse.* We were always traveling, doing interviews and research for her books. She had another one she was doing on the side about urban legends. We didn't have a home base, but we did have this motor home she'd converted to run mostly on solar energy. She was going to be an engineer before Midas."

She tapped the mat with a finger. "She did my bike, too, and made this for our computers."

"What happened?" He prompted. Maybe it wasn't polite to push her to talk about it, but maybe she'd been right about humans being inherently interested in each other. He wanted to know why Daisy didn't have a motor home. He wanted to know why she wasn't traveling with Violet Johansen.

Daisy ran a thumb over her laptop. "We ran into my uncle. He had kids, so there was this whole random part of my family I'd never met just...existing. I was excited to get to know them, but there was a caravan that was supposed to pass by through this desert about thirty miles out of town. I learned later that people tended to avoid that group. They were dangerous people.

"She asked me if I wanted to stay with my uncle while she met the caravan. I'd seen a couple of those before, so it wasn't as exciting as getting to know my family." She cleared her throat. "We, uh. We never found out what happened to her."

"I'm so sorry," Winter said. He knew the words weren't enough. They could never be enough. Maybe he'd been right in that way. But she'd been right too, because the words were all he had.

Daisy nodded, receiving his sympathy in silence. "I stayed with my uncle for about a year, hoping she would come back. Then I decided to finish her book for her. And...that's what I've been doing." She gave him half a smile. "But she never officially gave me permission to write it, so...'Unofficial'."

"I'm sorry if I've been hard on you," he said.

She shook her head. "You're just looking out for your town."

"Still..." he trailed off. What was he supposed to say? That he would've been gentler if he'd known she'd suffered a tragedy? Somehow he felt that wouldn't go over well. He wanted to help her, wanted to say *something* that would make her feel even a little bit better. That wasn't what he was good at, though. He protected people from physical threats, not emotional ones.

"Um," he cleared his throat nervously. "Do you, uh. Do you still want to interview me?"

Daisy's eyes snapped to his, and they were brighter than before. Just a little bit; like sunlight breaking through the clouds.

No Bones About It

The day that changed my life – and, honestly, that saved it – was the stereotypically perfect summer day. It was sunny; the only clouds in the sky were tufts of cotton floating in the blue. My parents had an old Volkswagen van that's air conditioning didn't work, so all the windows were down and the scent of fresh cut grass blew in as we cruised down the highway.

I was thirteen and my parents were taking me to a gun range for the first time. My dad had belonged to the gun club for twenty years at that point, but he's been shooting since he was even younger than I was. My mom has never been as passionate about it as my dad, but she enjoys it. Dad took us to the outside range, about half an hour outside the city where we lived. It was more of a glorified town, but we called it a city. The range was a clearing in thick woods about half as big as a football field with the shooting area itself backed up against a small hill.

The hill is a precaution. Bullets travel until they hit something, which *can* be the ground if they reach the end of their projectile curve first. That's unlikely, though. It's safer to have a mound of dirt between bullets and any people, even if there aren't supposed to be any people around for miles. A few hundred yards in front of the hill is a long, chest-height table. Well, for the average sized person it was about waist-high, but I was a short thirteen-year-old.

My dad showed me around a handgun that was small in his hands but relatively large in mine.

"This is called the safety," he said. "When it's on this side, it's safe. You can't fire the gun. You still shouldn't point it at anyone, but it shouldn't go off. When it's like this," he slid the safety back to reveal a long red strip. "It's live. That means you can pull the trigger and it'll shoot."

He'd told me all that before, but when you're dealing with lethal weaponry and teenagers you can never be too careful. He flipped the safety back on and showed me how to take out and load the magazine. It slid out the bottom of the grip and could hold twenty rounds. You have to put the bullets in one at a time, which my middle school brain thought took *forever.*

I finally slid it back into the gun with a satisfying click. My dad took the gun and pulled the top of it back.

"This is called a slide," he said. "You pull it back to load the bullets into the chamber. This is a semi-automatic pistol, so you only have to pull the slide back once after you load it. Now, this is important. Look at this."

I leaned forward obediently, watching as he detached the magazine and put it down on the table.

"Now it's not loaded, right?" He asked.

It looked empty to me, but I knew a trick question when I heard it. "No."

"Right, it's still loaded." He pulled the slide back again and tilted the gun until a bullet clattered to the table. "Always assume there's one in the chamber, Emery."

I nodded solemnly.

We shot off a bunch of rounds, aiming at paper targets, pyramids of empty pop cans, and a few old dinosaur toys. (My parents were of the opinion that all toys were gender neutral, so I played with Barbies *and* dinosaurs as a kid.) After I killed a t-rex for the fifth time, my dad told me to put the gun down and stay behind the counter (the "line") while he went to the bathroom. I ejected the magazine and stood back.

Mom wiggled her fingers at me and set up a large paper target in the shape of a person. She put it slightly closer than my targets and emptied her magazine into a close cropping around the chest. I watched her for a while, but when she started taking down the now very dead poster man my eyes wandered.

I gazed out at the field, taking in the wreckage of paper, cans, and figurines. The t-rex had landed next to something smooth and off-white peeking out of the grass. I squinted at it, but I couldn't make it out. Checking that Mom was still dealing with the paper man, I figured it was safe to take a look.

Thick green grass sprouted up around a tiny, half-demolished skeleton. I poked it with the toe of my sneaker, turning over a skull about the width of my palm but half the height. There was a ribcage, a wing bone, and half a leg.

I was fascinated. I stared at it, trying to imagine what it had been and why it had died. How long had it been there? What was its story? I felt something I'd never felt before building inside of me. An almost magnetic force drew me to it. I crouched down and, against all the advice I'd ever gotten about germs, ran my fingers over the tiny bones. It was like I was in a trance.

"*EMERY!*"

I fell over, startled.

Dad charged towards me and grabbed me by the arm, hoisting me up and dragging me back to the line. "*What were you thinking?!*"

He never yelled. I shrank into myself. "N-nothing I was just waiting for you!"

"I told you never to cross the line unless I tell you it's safe!" He shouted.

"It *was* safe!" I protested. "Mom wasn't shooting and I didn't have my gun—"

"And did you make sure your gun was *completely* empty before you walked in front of it?"

"Yes! I took the magazine out!" I pointed to it desperately.

Dad picked up the gun and pointed it at Mom's new target. From behind the line, she set her own weapon down to watch. He pulled the trigger. The sound of the shot was like thunder and I'd never seen anything as scary as the hole that appeared in the paper.

"W-w-w-how?" I squeaked in a weak voice.

Dad put a hand on my shoulder, leaning over to look me in the eyes. He wasn't yelling anymore but was just as desperate for me to understand. "There can always be one in the chamber, Emery. *Never* assume a gun isn't loaded."

That day I developed a healthy respect for both firearms and skeletal remains. Different types of respect, though. The respect for firearms was one born of fear and a recognition of power. The respect for the dead and what they leave behind was born of curiosity and love.

"So, what you're telling me is your first love was a tiny bird skeleton?" was Darren's response. He had one eyebrow lifted as well as the side of his mouth, making his whole face look tilted.

"I guess so," I said. Back then, I couldn't tell if it was friendly banter or a jibe, but I decided to give him the benefit of the doubt. After all, we'd worked together for ten years before ever meeting; our friendship was founded on strangeness.

Really, saying we work "together" is a stretch. The reason Darren and I never met before the gala where I regaled him with my origin story is because I work in a lab as an osteoarcheologist and he supervises and consults on digs around the world. As he crouches in ditches in countries whose language he doesn't speak, I analyze the skeletons and other artifacts discovered at the site. Despite the constant time zone changes, we've kept in contact after finally meeting in person at a gala put on by our employer, New York City's own Museum of Natural History.

Sometimes, when I'm really lucky, Darren tags along with the artifacts and visits me for a few days. He doesn't call ahead like a normal person because he thinks trying to scare me is funny. One time he ordered an extra box just so he could scream when I opened it. I almost stabbed him with a pen. So, when he sends me a text that he's on his way like a normal person, I can't help but be suspicious as I try to think of what dastardly trick he's planning. Then he sends me a list of the artifacts he's accompanying and I'm too busy prepping the lab to worry about it.

For the last year and a half, he's been on a dig in Central America. They've been unearthing the ruins of a completely buried city. The working theory is that a flood devastated the area and covered it in layers of sediment, but they haven't been able to confirm anything yet. Up until a few months ago, the only things they found were partial buildings and scattered objects. Then, almost as if they unlocked a new level in a video game, they started finding skeletons.

Unsurprisingly, my favorite things to look at are skeletons. Not only are they proof that living things existed in a certain place, but they tell epic stories about those things and the lives they led. I understand how they can make people uneasy, especially particularly empathetic people, because nobody wants to think of what they would look like reduced to that. Still for me, it's encouraging. The people whose skeletons I study can't speak for themselves anymore and we usually don't have anything they've written down, but their history is still preserved in their bones. Even thousands of years after the world they knew crumbled to dust, they are heard and remembered.

"Emerald!" Darren bursts through the doors, throwing his arms wide.

"Darry!" I jump up to give him a hug, using his shoulders to give me a bit of lift so I can peek around him at the boxes being carted in.

"I haven't even been here thirty seconds and you're already ignoring me?" He asks, faux whining.

"If you don't want to be ignored, don't bring such interesting company," I tease, squirming out of his grasp to follow the boxes.

"This is why you're still single," he says.

"I'm married to science. We're very happy together."

"I thought you were a Christian."

I snort. "The two aren't mutually exclusive, dummy. Just ask Einstein."

Long, thin boxes are being pushed forward on carts by delivery men with the logo of the museum sewn into their outfits. It's kind of like a parade of beggar's caskets and I feel a bit irreverent bouncing with excitement, but I figure these people have waited long enough to have their stories told. Maybe they'd be just as eager as me.

"I can't believe you found *five whole skeletons*!" I gush. "Wait – six? There are six boxes, I thought you only found five skeletons."

I glance back just in time to see Darren shrug. His hands are in the front pockets of his jeans and his eyes roam lazily over his delivery. "We found one more a few days before we were going to ship them out. It took a lot of work to get it out of the ground in time to join the others, so I hope you appreciate it."

"I definitely do!" I tie my hair up in a bun and head over to the sink to wash my hands. "This is going to be awesome! Grab some gloves, you can help!"

"No thanks," he laughs. "It's my first time back in the city in over a year, and not everyone prefers dead people to live ones."

I stick my tongue out at him and pull a set of gloves on. "I don't know if it's a preference so much as an appreciation for humans who aren't actively trying to hide who they are."

"Ugh, what a snob."

I roll my eyes and turn back to the deliveries, directing the workers on what to unload where. At some point during all this, Darren leaves. I'm not worried. He'll come back if I take too long and drag me off to do important human things like eating and relaxing. In the meanwhile, I'll do what I do best: talk to the dead.

Skeletons are much more detailed than people think. I've seen graphics where the same skeleton is pasted over and over but each iteration has a different label; male, female, Latinx, East Asian, etc. I know what the creators are trying to say, but the truth is that skeletal structure differs not only for gender, but also race and age. I never correct people, not wanting to make them feel bad, but secretly I think maybe they're going about it the wrong way. People aren't equally valuable because we're all the same. Part of the reason we're equally valuable is because we're all different. We're all one of a kind, and therefore all incredibly rare and immeasurably special.

The first thing I do is start taking photo and video like these are my six children, documenting every possible inch of them. After that, I take preliminary measurements before carefully collecting samples to run carbon dating on. Then I get out a microscope and a notebook and start looking them over, piece by piece, watching as their stories unfold before me. It's while I'm doing this that I find the first red flag.

In one episode of the American version of *The Office*, Jim talks about all the pranks he's pulled on Dwight. One of them involves putting little weights into Dwight's phone over time so he didn't notice a difference, then taking them all out. Because Dwight was used to the phone being heavy, he used as much force as he would to lift that weight and ended up hitting himself in the face.

That's basically what happens when I grab the skull from the sixth skeleton. It practically flies off the table, startling me. I narrow my eyes at it as if I can intimidate it into telling me what just happened. Lifting it up and down experimentally, I can't ignore the odd lightness. Just to be sure I'm not making stuff up, I grab Skull #5 in my other hand. Yeah, something is definitely up with Skull #6.

Repeating the experiment with the rest of the bones forces me to update my hypothesis; something is definitely up with Skeleton #6.

My first thought is this is Darren's new prank, but closer inspection reveals these are definitely human remains. I don't like where my mind is going, but I hate having to wait at least a day for the carbon dating results just to confirm it. Actually... I grab a few extra samples from Skeleton #6 and stick them in the spectrometer. If the suspicion in the back of my mind is right, I know I won't believe it without a second opinion.

A lot of human remains aren't technically fossils. The term "fossil" is supposed to refer to preserved matter at least ten thousand years old. Anything younger than that is slightly different. There are a few methods of preservation, but the most common one is called permineralization. It's when minerals seep into pores in the bone and solidify. Here's the kicker: these permineralized bones are about thirty percent heavier than a normal, non-preserved bone. Bones that aren't preserved decompose within twenty years. These two facts do not weave a nice narrative in my head.

Part of me wants to stare at the spectrometer until I get the results, but I force myself to go back to my apartment. I've been told I have a sixth sense for archaeology that steers me like a compass towards details others might miss. Up until tonight, when I'm stuck staring at the ceiling for five hours trying to convince myself I'm wrong, I took it as a compliment.

"Emery?" When Darren pokes me in the side, I jump about a foot in the air. "What's wrong?" He asks, laughing.

"Uuuuuh." I clear my throat and swivel in the chair to give him a better view of the computer screen. "Take a look at this."

He rests an elbow on my shoulder as he leans over and squints at the data. As he reads, I watch his face. Passive curiosity gives way to surprise. He drops his arm from my shoulder and leans even closer to the screen. Though his face is illuminated by the blue light, it seems to grow darker. All traces of humor leave him.

"Is this right?"

I bite back the instinctive retort at the audacity of someone questioning my work because under the circumstances, I would've asked the same thing. I *did* ask the same thing. I nod, crossing my arms over my chest and looking back at the screen.

"Yeah. I ran another test on a separate sample just to be sure." After a tense moment of silence, I take a deep breath. "You know what this means, right?"

"Enlighten me." His voice is almost a growl, but I don't blame him. This would not be how I'd want to spend my first week home, either.

"According to the carbon dating, this skeleton is almost a thousand years younger than the others. In fact, it probably only *became* a skeleton within the last year or so."

"It was always a skeleton, it just had meat around it before," he murmurs.

At any other time, I'd roll my eyes. "I took a look back over it, and I'm almost one-hundred percent certain the cause of death was blunt force trauma. Which means this person was probably murdered and dumped at the dig site so the crime wouldn't be discovered."

"Or they could've just fallen and hit their head!" He snaps, straightening up. "Don't go throwing the word 'murder' around like that. Are you *trying* to start something?"

"*I* didn't start anything; *I* didn't kill this guy." I glare up at him. "And yeah, sure it's possible that he hit his head on a rock, but if you compare his skeleton to the others found at the site, they're almost identical to the untrained eye, besides the fact that the victim's skeleton isn't permineralized. That means someone did a little Hollywood touch up on the bones post-mortem. *That* couldn't have been a rock."

Darren curses and glares daggers at the skeleton, which is still lying on the examination table. He breathes in through his nose a few times before turning back to me. "Alright, here's what we're going to do: you catalogue everything you can about the...*victim*, and I'll go tell Joanna."

Joanna Oliver is my boss, the museum director. She coordinates with digs around the world, including Darren's. I've never seen her at a loss for what to do, and I'd love to have her down here to direct me, but...

"Why can't we just call the police?" I ask.

He massages his forehead. "Because the murder didn't take place in this country. It's not in the local PD's jurisdiction. Joanna can probably get in contact with someone at the FBI or whichever bureau deals with international crime."

"Good point." I turn back to the computer and create a new folder. "Go get Joanna; I'll be here."

I transfer everything I already have on the skeleton – the murder victim – from the folder where I'm storing information about the other skeletons, then get up and circle the table.

Murder investigations are different than osteoarcheological investigations, but at their cores the two are very similar. You want to look at the body and the evidence and find out everything you can about who you found, what they did, how they lived, how they fit into society, and how they died. Murder investigations are a little more intense, though. You've got to figure it out quickly. I've already figured out cause of death, gender, age, race, and I've even gotten a window of fatality established, or whatever it's called. I tilt my head at the skeleton, considering the idea that just popped into my brain.

I wash my hands and grab some new gloves, then head over to the table with a magnifying glass. In order for the skeleton to have been mistaken for one of the others, it can't have had any flesh or organs in it. An exposed body can turn to pure bone within ten days, but there are plenty of ways to get "the meat", as Darren put it, off the bone more quickly. The easiest and fastest way involves soaking or boiling it in water, but that won't do anything to the brain. If the killer didn't want to leave the body out in the open and wait around, they would have had to get the brain out a different way.

Egyptians, when mummifying corpses, would stick tools up the nasal cavity to remove the brain. It takes a long time if you're doing it right. Even then, people who aren't trained have a high chance of accidentally performing a post-mortem facelift. Unless we're dealing with a serial killer who has both that unique skillset and *lots* of practice, there should be marks from the tools. I wasn't looking for it before, but now that I am it's obvious; the nasal cavity is absolutely covered in spiderweb cracks. Bits and pieces have actually been knocked loose. The killer probably didn't care too much about being careful, assuming any damage would be chalked up to thousands of years underground.

The thrill that courses through me now is something I've never felt before. It's like the excitement of finding something unexpected on an artifact, but with an almost vindictive twist. *You thought you were free and clear, didn't you?* I think about the murderer and bare my teeth in a grin. *You thought wrong.*

When Darren gets back and knocks on the door, I feel like I'm waking up from a trance. I've been so deep in the zone that I forgot about the existence of time and space outside this lab. My eyes flutter like I'm trying to blink sleep from them and I look slowly from Darren to the clock. It's been *hours.*

My face wrinkles as I frown. "What took you so long? Where's Joanna?"

He brushes long bangs out of his face, smoothing his hair back. "She's been on the phone with the FBI for hours now and had me doing the same thing with my boss down at the site. This is going to be a big, annoying deal."

"Murder investigations can be *so* inconvenient," I joke.

"You're telling me. Anyway, I just came down here to tell you the FBI's not sending any agents down until tomorrow, so we're free to go. As long as you're finished with what you're doing...?" He raises an eyebrow and looks over the mess I've made of the lab.

"Uh..." Before I answer, I grab a legal pad from the counter. When I was trying to get started, ideas were just exploding in my brain like fireworks. I had to write them down or risk spinning my wheels, trapped in hypotheticals in my head. Scanning the list, I nod slowly. "Yeah, I think I'm good. I've got a few samples being processed, but the machines turn themselves off once they're done and feed the data directly to the computer, so I can sort through it tomorrow."

"Great." He offers a smile. "Let's grab some pizza and head back to your place. I was thinking I'd stay over for a few days."

I peel off the gloves and raise an eyebrow at him. "Why? I thought you were staying in your cousin's place while she's in France."

"Yeah, but I figured it would be safer...you know." He's rubbing the back of his neck, trying to be casual about it.

"Safer?"

"Well, someone obviously went through a lot of trouble to cover up the murder and you just ruined everything for them, so..." He bites his lip and smiles again, apologetic. "It's probably stupid; they probably have no idea you exist, but I'd feel better if you weren't alone."

"That's okay." I wave him off. A pod of fear is blooming inside me, but like he said, it's ridiculous. "I'll be fine. You go home; enjoy sleeping in your own bed."

"At least let me buy you something to eat," he counters. "I feel terrible, you should have gone home hours ago. I can't imagine how hungry you must be."

"I'm not, actually." I think I *was* hungry, before he brought all this up. Now all I want to do is go home and lock myself in my bedroom in my locked apartment in my secured building. I try to shake off the thought. I'm not going to overreact like a kid walking past a graveyard in October.

"If you're sure..." he caves reluctantly.

"I'm sure." I have a marksmanship medal from college and a PhD. I'll be fine.

As a woman, feeling my hackles rise when I'm walking alone at night is normal, but tonight the danger feels more imminent. How did this happen? I'm suddenly in the middle of an *international murder investigation*. Am I going to have to talk to someone from MI6? Wait, no. The murder happened in Central America. Am I going to have to talk to someone from...NAFTA?

I don't even feel safe in my car. I find myself checking the backseat for stowaways every time I stop at a sign or a red light. An irrational fear that someone's using the clutter as camouflage won't leave me alone, even though logically there's very little chance a whole person can be hiding under a sweatshirt, twelve CD's, and a snow shovel.

Calm down, I think to myself sharply. *You're overreacting*. After all, what are the odds that the killer is even in this country, let alone watching me? Just because examining the skeleton today has been a huge event in my life doesn't mean everyone else's world has irrevocably changed.

I manage to convince myself that I'm catastrophizing by the time I get home. I park on the street in front of my building and run inside, my hands only shaking a little bit as I key in the code for the building. I close the apartment door behind me, lock it with more force than necessary, and lean back against it. A weight lifts from my chest and my bravado returns immediately. There's nothing to worry about. Whoever the killer is doesn't even know who I am. I've never even *met* any other members of the dig team.

I feel silly for freaking out all the way home, but I don't berate myself for it. My body is flooding with relief or some sort of post-adrenaline high. I decide to run myself a hot bath and mix a cappuccino using my actual espresso machine. I've earned it after today. As the bath is filling up, I head back to the kitchen to get started on the coffee.

The note is in the middle of my table. I generally only use it for breakfast; eating lunch at work and being too tired from my day to not eat on the couch for supper. The note is typed out on a page that's been ripped in half. The font is normal, the same one that pops up when I open the word processor at work. For all its seeming innocuousness, the message makes my whole body tense up, like it's getting ready to fight or flee.

{Keep your mouth shut}

How can four words change everything? In the same way a simple carbon dating scan and improperly weighted bone can, I suppose.

I'm definitely not taking a bath anymore. In fact, I don't think I'm going to sleep at all. Instead of making a cappuccino, I brew a pot of extra-strong coffee. As it percolates, I dig out the box set of *Bones* I got for Christmas two years ago. I drink coffee and watch almost the full first season before it's time to go to work. I wonder if any of the crime-solving in there would work in real life. I tell myself it will. I tell myself I'm more prepared. I tell myself that being more prepared makes me less nervous.

I'm lying.

Before I leave, I take my gun out of the safe under my bed and put it in my purse. Dad bought it for me when I moved out, and since then I've only been to the range a handful of times. He told me I was a natural, and I hope he was being honest and not just seeing my abilities with rose-colored goggles because I'm his daughter.

I can't focus on my work, which makes me angry. I love my work. I sit around for almost an hour, not wanting to get in the middle of anything in case the FBI shows up. Nothing irritates me more than having to shift gears in the middle of an activity or project. Anxiety itches under my skin and I finally open up a report hoping some activity will relieve the tension. It doesn't. In fact, the frustration that builds when I can't concentrate just makes it worse. By the time Darren shows up, I'm starting to wish I would've read more about the science of spontaneous combustion.

"Hey," he says, waving.

"FBI isn't here yet," I reply in greeting.

He looks sheepish. "Yeah, Joanna told me to let you know they can't come until tomorrow."

"*What*?!" I slam a fist on the desk. "Didn't she tell them about the skeleton?!"

"It's the government, Em. They're probably still stuck in red tape."

I shut down my computer and get up. "Let's take our lunch."

He smirks. "It's ten in the morning."

"Congratulations, you can tell time. Let's go." I grab my purse and head out the door. Darren laughs a little and closes it, following on my heels.

"That doesn't definitively prove anything, though," Darren says after I tell him about the note.

"It proves enough!"

We're strolling down the street much too casually for my taste. Clutching the strap of my purse to keep my hands from shaking, I narrow my eyes at him. How dare he be so cool and composed while I'm panicking! His eyes drift back to me and I quickly assume a neutral expression.

"So..." he begins. "What do you want to do?"

Oh, yeah. It's my life at stake, I should probably take a more active role in trying to...unstake it. I drum my fingers on my purse strap and cast my eyes skyward like there's going to be an answer written in the clouds.

"Well," I start thinking out loud just so he doesn't accidentally interrupt. "I probably don't want to go back to my apartment, which sucks because my car is there and you don't drive."

"You didn't drive to work?"

"I stayed up all night. Driving tired is basically driving drunk and all that." I shouldn't feel so annoyed at having to explain my thought process to someone who's not in my head, but I am *stressed* and everything is getting on my last nerve.

"Fair enough. So, you're thinking we should run?"

"I'm thinking if someone's trying to kill me, I want to be as far away from them as I can."

"Good point."

Regardless of the lovely honors I graduated with, I'm coming up with nothing. But being outside is sending prickles across my skin, like thousands of eyes are watching me from every direction.

"Let's go somewhere..." My historian's mind wants to say 'defensible', but that's a pretty militaristic term and right now I'm still hoping we can somehow work this out non-violently. "...not outside," I finish lamely. "Where we can see someone if they're coming."

"Good thinking." He flashes me one of those dimpled grins. "You sure you're not secretly a spy?"

I snort. "If I was secretly a spy, I wouldn't be so worried about someone threatening me." I spin around. We're about half a block from the museum, which is not great. If I was trying to hunt someone down and she wasn't at her apartment, I'd definitely stake out her work next.

"Let's head into the city," I say out loud, pulling out my phone.

Darren compliments my ideas again as I search for a Starbucks on my favorite maps app. There's one a few blocks away, but I find myself leaning towards the one almost twice the distance from where we are in the interest of avoiding anyone who might want to kill us. To me, Starbucks has a Beat Poet vibe. It's slick and modern, but also laid-back and chill. I can't decide whether to pace myself to make my iced Americano last longer or to chug it so I can get a burst of adrenaline.

"Alright, the FBI agent isn't coming until tomorrow," I say. "Which means we have to survive the rest of today, tonight, and coming to work tomorrow."

"That's assuming that the killer will just let it go after we talk to the FBI agent," Darren points out. He stirs the froth into his latte.

"Why would they bother trying to kill us if we've already told the FBI everything we know?"

"Revenge," he points out.

"Ah." Embarrassingly enough, I forgot that was a thing. "They can give us protection though, can't they?"

"Sure." He takes a sip of his drink. "As long as the government hasn't asked them to cut down on spending."

I throw my hands up and make a face at him. "Aren't *you* just Mr. Sunshine?"

"That's what they call me." He leans forward. "Look, I think what we need to do is get out of town. We can rent a cabin or something in a place neither of us have been before, then call Joanna from there and get her to send the FBI up to us."

I nod even as I ask, "What if they need us to clarify stuff with the skeleton?"

"Then they and their guns can escort us back to the museum."

"Alright, I'll give you that." I lean back in my chair and lift the straw to my lips.

As I do, I gaze around at the other patrons as inconspicuously as I can. As far as I can tell, none of them are paying any particular attention to us. Of the people I noticed who came in closely after us, most took their orders to go. Two old ladies who were right behind us in line have commandeered a small table. They don't look particularly suspicious. Four kids who are probably in college, considering the time of day, are all seated at the bar. None of them have turned around for ten minutes so they're not watching us.

A mysterious, broody man in a black hoodie is sitting in an armchair near the false fireplace, eyeing up everyone else just like I am. He'd be the most suspicious, but his aesthetic tells me he's not our guy. He's got bottle black hair carefully gelled to keep his bangs over one of his eyes, heavy guyliner, a diamond lip piercing, and a silver chain choker. His hoodie sleeves are pushed up to his elbows, revealing wristbands and bracelets thick around his thin wrists. His skin is vampire-pale.

The dig site is in Central America. If he was the killer, he'd be at least a little tan from being out in the summer sun. His eyes are brown, so I know he's not an albino. And with the effort he's put into his appearance, I can't picture him creeping up to a dig site at night to hide a skeleton in the dirt.

"So, how are we getting out to this cabin?" I ask.

Darren starts tracing a line on the table like he's running his finger along an invisible map. "We take the subway over to the edge of the city, then call a taxi from the last stop. It'll be cheaper than calling someone from here."

It's nice of him to think about budgeting when we're about to be murdered.

"Okay. Sounds like a plan. Let's go." I slurp up the rest of my coffee and hop to the floor.

The caffeine hits my system fast and I feel an overwhelming urge to try and make a basket with my ice-filled cup from across the room. I hold myself back, though. No need to make any more enemies than necessary.

We make it to the subway without incident, though every second I'm expecting to feel a knife through my ribs from behind. The throng of pedestrians on the sidewalk is claustrophobic and the espresso in my blood merges with the anxiety to paint me a fantasy about shoving everyone away from me, some into the flow of traffic, and screaming so loud the entire world goes silent. *Simmer down, Emery,* I tell myself.

We're in line to buy our tickets when Darren presses closer to me and leans over to whisper, "Hey."

"What? What's wrong?" I start looking around.

He laughs softly. "No, no, nothing's wrong. I just think...do you still have your...you know...*paperweight*?"

"Yeah." My hand drifts to my purse, which suddenly feels heavier when I remember the gun. It only takes two seconds to envision a future where we're caught with a gun in the subway, arrested, and thrown into prison for life. If caffeine is going to mess with my nerves this much, why does it taste so good? That's not fair.

"Why don't you give me the magazine? That way, if we get caught, you can show them that it's not loaded."

I want it to be loaded, though. If there's some mysterious killer coming after me, I prefer to have a loaded weapon. However, going to jail doesn't sound fun, either

"I'll give it back to you after we get out of the subway," he says.

I sigh. "Fiiiine." I reach into my bag and detach the magazine without looking, sliding it up my sleeve before holding my hand out to Darren like I want to shake on something.

He takes my hand curiously, but understanding washes over his face when he feels the metal press into his palm. He hides it behind his wrist and shoves his hand into one of his insanely deep man pockets.

We make it onto the subway and scoot to the back of the car. There are no actual seats left, so we settle for the aisle. I hang onto a bar and Darren grabs one of the rungs. It seems to take forever for the train to lurch into motion. Speed has never felt more soothing.

I can't turn my brain off, though. Something's bugging me. That seems like the understatement of the century, considering the situation. Still, it's like...an itch at the back of my mind. Eerily similar to the itch I felt when I was examining the skeleton for the first time. Something's just not adding up. I go over the information again, slower.

The train hits a bump and jolts, and it's like the motion shakes the idea loose. *How did the killer get from the dig site to the museum?*

How did they know where the skeletons were going? How did they know about me, *specifically?*

A horrible suspicion rears up in the back of my mind. I hate myself for even considering it, but can I afford not to? It takes me a minute to come up with how I can test my growing theory, and another to figure out how to word it so it's not immediately obvious what I'm thinking. Especially considering how ashamed I'll be if I'm wrong.

{Hey Joanna,} I type out the text with one hand, still gripping the railing with the other. {When's the FBI going to show up?}

Half a minute later I get a response, the notification sound lost among the chaos around us.

{LOL!} Weird start to a message regarding a murder investigation, but okay. {I'm not worried about you taking a longer lunch than normal. I know Darren just got in. Have fun!}

I slide my phone back into my purse, feeling numb. Obviously, Joanna doesn't know she was supposed to call the FBI. She probably doesn't even know why she would. My feelings about Darren's presence abruptly shift. Like finally seeing through an illusion, the aura of protection turns sickly and sinister and I realize that I've made a big mistake. The subway suddenly feels like a sardine can, the walls pressing together and forcing me way too close to him.

As if he heard my thoughts, he looks at me over his shoulder. "You doing alright back there, Em?" He sounds so concerned and caring.

It sends shivers up my spine.

"I'm fine," I say, heart pounding. I know I can't hide my emotions for to save my life — bad phrasing — so I've got to be smart about this. I lean into the fear and tell the truth. "I just can't believe this is happening, you know?"

His eyebrows draw together, lips pursing in a sympathetic smile. "I know. But it'll be over soon."

"Yeah." I feel like I just found a bomb with a digital countdown. *Soon.*

The subway screeches to a halt and we join the other people swarming into the station. I could try to lose him in the crowd, but right now the only advantage I have is that he doesn't know that I'm trying to get away from him. I need to be smart. I keep up with him as we start towards the stairs. As usual, he's so sure of himself. Natural. Maybe that should've tipped me off a long time ago. What normal person looks *natural* in a situation like this?

Looking around for an excuse, I catch sight of a sign for public toilets. It's right next to the stairs with an arrow pointing deeper into the tunnel. *Perfect.* I grab his arm and lean around him, trying not to shudder as we touch.

"I have to use the bathroom," I say, indicating the sign.

For the first time, he looks a little frustrated. "Now?"

"Yeah." I give him a weak smile and press my hands against my stomach. "When I'm nervous, my digestive system gets a little..." I trail off meaningfully.

He makes a face. "Fine. Be quick, though. We need to keep moving if we're going to stay ahead of the killer."

"Right." I nod resolutely and start down the tunnel, following the sign.

New York subways aren't as crowded as I thought when I was a kid, but right now that's not helpful. If it was like that scene in *Crocodile Dundee,* Darren would make a lot of people mad if he tried to chase me. In reality, there's plenty of space for people to weave around each other.

Is he watching me? My neck and shoulders tingle, but I can't tell if it's my sixth sense or just paranoia. The bathroom is just up on my left. I don't have a lot of time to decide what I'm going to do; either I pass the bathroom, or I go in and try to think up a plan. If he's watching me, he'll know I'm trying to get away if I keep walking. But maybe he'll be watching the door if I go in. Or...I wonder if he'll look away for a minute, anticipating me taking a while. That could be my shot.

I duck into the bathroom.

I wander over to the sinks and turn one on. I can pretend to wash my hands so I don't look like a creeper if anyone comes in. Looking at myself in the dingy mirror, I suddenly remember the video I saw where a former government agent critiqued disguises in movies. She said the most important thing to do when disguising yourself is remove the biggest identifiers. For example, if they're looking for a brunette in a blue jacket and glasses, putting on a wig and ditching the jacket and glasses will throw them off.

I put my purse down and start digging through it. I take out my wallet and phone, laying them on the counter so I can dig around the bottom. Score! A purple scrunchie. *Why do I have a purple scrunchie?* Doesn't matter. I put my hair up in a bun and look over my outfit.

A long-sleeved blue t-shirt and bootcut jeans. I pull my arms out of the sleeves and try to stick them out the collar. I hear it tear a little as I force it over my shoulders, but that's fine. It's for a good cause – namely, me staying alive. I tie the sleeves around my neck to make it look like a halter top. On close inspection, it's clearly a scrap job. But hopefully it'll pass if anyone's watching from a distance. I crouch to roll my jeans up as high as I can and look myself over.

I'm obviously still me. Hopefully just because I know what I've done. I turn off the facet just as the door swings open. I jump about a foot in the air before I realize it's another woman. She gives me a cursory glance as she makes a beeline for a stall. I catalogue her outfit almost subconsciously; gray windbreaker, black dress pants, large red crocodile skin bag.

"Hey!" I shout.

She flinches, turning to narrow her eyes at me.

I hold my hands up in what's hopefully a peaceful sign. "Will you trade purses with me for…" Luckily, we stopped at the ATM earlier in the interest of staying under the radar. "…two hundred dollars?"

Her eyes widen and flit to my purse. "Why?" she asks warily.

"I just…" What response would sound the least crazy? Or criminal? 'I swear it's not drugs' probably won't come off as reassuring as I'm hoping. "I really like your bag."

She looks me over carefully. "Cash?"

"Yeah!" I snatch my wallet from the counter and fumble with the zipper before I finally get it open. Pulling out the money, I hand it over to her.

She counts it carefully, then slides her bag off her shoulder. Swallowing a relieved laugh which would definitely come off as unhinged, I grab all my stuff out of my purse and put it on the counter. I see her jerk away and realize too late I just whipped out a gun with no warning.

"Waitwaitwait!" I grab it by the barrel. "It's not loaded! See? No magazine!" I stick my finger in the empty cavity of the gun.

Her face is pale and her eyes dart around like a scared rabbit's. I toss the gun back on the counter and put my hands up again. She slowly edges back towards the sink. Without taking her eyes off me, she snatches my purse up, tosses her stuff inside, and practically runs out of the bathroom. I grimace. I hope she didn't really have to go.

As I start dumping my stuff in the red purse, I take a little comfort in the fact that giving the magazine to Darren helped in this instance. Mostly I still feel like an idiot for falling for his tricks. Last but not least, I grab the gun itself. I hesitate, hook a finger in the waistband of my jeans, and tug. Unfortunately, they're too tight for me to use the TV cop method. Reluctantly, I stick it in the bag. I won't be able to whip it out at a moment's notice. Unless...I hook one strap over my shoulder and leave the other one hanging at my side. At least this way I'll be able to reach inside more easily. *Alright.* Taking a deep breath, I square my shoulders. *Better not wait till he's looking for me.*

I duck out the door and take a sharp left, heading away from the stairs. The amount of effort it takes just to walk normally is unbelievable. Normally I hate cardio, but right now all I want to do is sprint as far as I can. I can't even look back to see if he's buying it, because then he could see my face.

Walking! I remember suddenly that the agent on the video said changing your stride helps a lot. Actually, I've noticed how I walk before; it's almost like an abortive runway stride. I step forward and in, like I'm going to cross one foot in front of the other, but stop right before they actually cross. Careful not to change my walking speed, I angle my feet out and try to step closer in line to my shoulders. After a while, I start to feel it in my hips. Have I discovered a new workout routine? *I'll come up with a clever name and patent the style. The tagline can be something like: increase calories burned while walking by something-something percent! I'll be rich.*

All I have to do is survive first.

I turn onto the next staircase I pass and take the steps two at a time. If Darren's still where he was before, he shouldn't be able to see me from this angle. Emerging into the street sends a surge of relief through me. Car exhaust and hot dogs have never smelled so good. I make a beeline away from the subway, eying everyone I pass with suspicion.

So. There's good news and bad news. The good news is I know who's coming after me. The bad news is he knows where I live. I could just go to the cops. Now that I know what's up, I can give them the full story. They'll have to believe it... I review the pieces I have in my head and frown. Aggravatingly enough, most of it is what my sister, who plays a cop on TV, would call circumstantial evidence. Like how figuring out a suspect went to the same party as the victim the night they died doesn't necessarily mean that suspect is the killer.

Shuddering, I think, *I really need to stop thinking about murder.*

But...who else would help? Who else *can* help? As I peek into my new bag to check that my gun is still there, the scent of rose perfume clocks me in the nose. With it comes my answer.

When I first moved to the city, my parents came over to my apartment often. It meant a lot, especially considering Mom absolutely hates city driving. They still come up any time I ask be-cause, as they like to remind me, I'm still their little girl. It was a rough adjustment at first, made even harder by me trying too hard to be independent.

One day, I locked my keys in my car and ended up stranded in a parking lot for five hours as I tried to get help. The first thing I did, of course, was try to break in using stuff from my purse like any reasonable person would. It took me the full first hour to give up on that. Then I called three locksmiths, none of whom were available, and finally I called the police. A squad car showed up and the policeman used only slightly better tools than I had. It took him about half an hour.

When I told my parents about it later, expecting them to laugh at the comedy of errors like I (eventually) had, they got upset. Mom asked me why I hadn't just called them to come help.

My mind went blank. I hadn't even considered that as an option, even though it would've taken way less time. They only live about two hours from the city, and though they don't have an extra car key, they have an extra apartment key. We could've just gone to my apartment, gotten my spare car keys, and opened the car no problem.

Well, I'm not going to make the same mistake twice. I hole up in a locally owned coffee shop/bar and call my parents.

"Hi there, honey!" Mom says cheerfully.

I hate to spoil her mood, but... "Hey Mom, can you or Dad come get me? I'll text you the address."

"Sure hon. Lock your keys in your car again?"

"Not exactly." Like I've been doing since I got here, I take a minute to scan the other patrons. "I'll tell you all about it later, but I need you to come get me right now."

"Why? What's going on?"

I know keeping her in the dark is just going to make her worry, but I don't think telling her is going to help. "I'll tell you when you get here. Just please come."

"Of course, sweetheart. I'll be right there." She sounds scared and I hate it.

"Thanks. I love you."

"I love you, too."

I hang up and sigh, putting my head down on the table. I wonder if I can just fall asleep here and wake up in a hundred years like Rip Van Winkle. I'll open my eyes and everyone will be speaking French, talking about the latest election of the Prime Minister of our beloved homeland, South Canada.

I force myself to sit up and keep looking around. Being aware of my surroundings and all that. This place is a large room on the ground floor of a commercial building, most of which is dedicated to local businesses. This particular business is partially bisected by a wall, leaving one side facing the street and one side almost hidden from the front window.

The coffee shop stretches from that wall up to that window, full of round light-brown wood tables and bare bulbs on the ceiling. There's a counter and bakery case right next to the door. Even at four in the afternoon, there are people hanging out in this section. Two hipsters bent over a game of Scrabble, steaming mugs of tea at their elbows. A man gazing seriously at his laptop as his fingers fly across the keys.

The bar itself is along the wall you can see from the coffee shop, but behind the partition are smooth, black gloss tables and egg-shaped chairs. It's darker, with bulbs in the ceiling covered with clouded glass to soften the light. There's also a kitchen tucked into the back wall where you can get actual restaurant food. I've never been in that section. Not to eat, that is. The bathrooms are over there.

I like this place. I like the juxtaposition of the homey, rustic café and the elegant dining area. Sometimes I come down here just to hang out and read a book. I've introduced it to most of my friends. Of course, I haven't made many new friends since those first few years and I think I've shown them all by now. Actually, the last person I introduced this place to was—

Darren.

The temperature seems to drop ten degrees as the memory comes back. I dragged him here, running my mouth about all sorts of things; personal stuff that I feel sick knowing he knows. I told him this was my favorite place in the city.

I can't stay *here*! It's the first place he'll look! I get up in a hurry, opening my phone to text Mom a new address. As I open the front door, I look up and down the street and he's *right there*. Half a block down on the left, heading my way.

I turn right and start running.

I realize immediately that I should've just gone back inside and hung around a group of people so he couldn't get at me without causing a scene. It's too late now. I pour on the speed and keep running, darting through the crosswalk just as the little person changes to a hand commanding me to stop. I hear honking and squealing brakes behind me and look over my shoulder, a sick hope in my chest that he got hit trying to come after me. I turn just in time to see him vault over the hood of another car and make it to the sidewalk. I swear internally and keep running.

I can run for a long time, especially when motivated. I was in cross country in high school. Here's the difference between cross country and track: cross country runners can keep a steady pace for a long time, but track runners can go fast. I am not fast.

A rough hand grabs my shoulder and yanks me backwards. The world blurs as I spin and suddenly I'm being slammed up against a wall. Darren's eyes are wild and fierce as he looks at me.

"Think you're—" he starts to say.

I'm not in a listening mood and I drop to the ground, kicking at one of his legs. He moves out of the way, but that gives me an opening to get up and run. I only make it a few feet before I realize we're in an alley. When he pulled me in here, I wasn't thinking of the environment, only escape. There were two directions for me to go, and I picked the one that leads to a dead end.

I'm not superstitious, but—

He grabs me around the waist, but I throw my hips back and my upper body forward and manage to break free. Of course, now I'm on the ground and he's towering above me like some sort of movie villain. I scramble backwards, reaching into my purse and pulling out the gun. Instinctively, he hesitates.

I get to my feet, still training the gun on him. "*Stay back!*" I yell. My voice sounds shrill. "*Stay back! I will shoot!*"

I went to a self-defense workshop where we were advised to yell things like "Drop your weapon" and "I will shoot" because it draws the attention of bystanders. Preferably bystanders who want to post something cool on the internet. Nobody did anything when Darren pulled me in here, but now there are a few people peering in curiously.

Darren laughs. "With what?" He pulls the magazine out of his pocket and dangles it in between us. "This?"

I flick the safety off. "*I'm not kidding, stay back!*"

He takes a confident step forward.

I pull the trigger.

The bullet hits him in the right shoulder, throwing him to the ground. He grabs at it, stunned as blood pours from the wound. Vaulting over his body in a jump that would make those track and field kids jealous, I sprint for the end of the open street.

Before I get there, a policeman comes jogging over, one hand on his walkie talkie and the other holding his own gun. I stop short, dropping the gun and putting my hands up – I did not come this far just to get shot by a good guy. The cop looks between me and Darren as a few helpful Instagrammers fill him in, offering their phones.

Darren's eyes are already dilated, shock setting in. He looks at me, confused. "How...?" he croaks.

Exhausted, I lean back on the wall he tried to pin me against just a few minutes ago. "There's always one in the chamber, Darren."

By the time Mom picks me up from the police station, it's almost midnight. I had to give statements upon statements, talk to my lawyer to make sure I don't get sued for defending myself with a firearm, wait around for the FBI to show up to talk about the skeleton, tell the CSI people how to get the data from my files at work, then get debriefed by the precinct captain.

She was a nice woman with a kind face, even if it did have a scar through half of it. I could tell she had a good sense of humor because the lipstick on one side of her scar was light pink while the lipstick on the other was brick red. She told me she wasn't supposed to give out information on active cases but knew how it felt to be left in suspense after an incident like this.

McDonald's is open all night, so Mom takes me there for ice cream just like she used to when I was a kid. I remember getting a chocolate cone when my best friend of three years moved out of state, a marble sundae when I bombed a test I'd spent the weekend studying for, and an Oreo blizzard when I found out the boy who had promised to wait until I was sixteen to go out with me (the age limit my parents had set) was seeing someone else in the meantime.

I swirl my straw around to mix the whipped cream into the mocha frappe, sitting cross-legged on the passenger seat.

"How are you doing, honey?" Mom asks gently.

I shrug.

She puts a hand on my knee. "Do you want to go back to your apartment or come home with me?"

"We wouldn't get home until, like, two AM," I mutter.

"That's okay with me."

Tears prick at the corners of my eyes. Fear and adrenaline kept me going through the whole incident, and afterwards I managed to ignore everything outside answering questions and following directions like a robot. Now, in the calm after the storm, the pain and betrayal is kicking in.

"I wanna go home," I whine like a little kid.

"Okay, sweetheart, we can do that."

Sadness flips to anger, as it so often does. I slam a fist down on my thigh, which doesn't hurt nearly enough.

"Emery!"

"Why am I so *stupid*?!" I demand, looking up at her with eyes blazing. "You never liked Darren, why couldn't *I* see that he was a psychopath?!"

"I didn't see this coming, either," she says. "I don't think anyone did. Do you think they would've let him have access to all those sharp archeological tools if they knew he was homicidal?"

"He used a tire iron," I mumble.

"Did he?" That's not the point and we both know it.

"I know, right?" I laugh bitterly. "Like, is there a more cliché way to kill someone with blunt force trauma?"

"Yeah, get a life, man," Mom agrees.

I rub at my eyes. "The guy was a protestor. He hated that foreigners were digging around in his country like they owned the place and carting off their history. Darren caught him trying to sabotage some equipment in the middle of the night and got the tire iron from his car. He followed the guy into the jungle when he went to sneak off and killed him once they were out of earshot of the dig site."

"That's horrible."

"It is. He just wanted to protect his history; he wasn't even trying to hurt anyone." Tears are coming, and I hate that not even half of them are for the victim. "How could he do this to me?" I wonder. "I thought we were friends."

Mom holds me for a while as I cry. It's a little awkward with the console between us, but that doesn't matter. Of all the things that are wrong right now, that's the lowest on the list. My head still seems to fit in the crook of her shoulder.

"What if I keep attracting people like Darren?" I ask, exhausted. "How do I know if I can trust anyone? Why do living people lie so much?"

She rubs my back. "Not everyone is like Darren. If they were, the world population would be a lot lower."

I laugh wetly and feel her jaw shift as she smiles.

"I don't know why people lie so much, but I'm not worried about you. After all, you figured out that Darren was a bad guy all on your own. He might have fooled you at first, but he couldn't fool you for long. And when he tried to hurt you, you stopped him. I don't think you should let this make you scared. I think you should let it fill you with confidence instead."

"Hmm." I turn that idea over in my mind, analyzing it like it's an artifact. It has at least some truth to it, and that's enough to make me believe there's a little hope. "I think I still like dead people more. They always tell the truth."

She sighs. "I hope this isn't because I let you play in the graveyard when you were little."

I blink. "I'm sorry, you *what*?"

One Does Not Simply Taxi into Mordor

In a world of science and magic, the possibilities are nearly endless. You can double-major in physics and alchemy. You can scubadive with mermaids. You can carpool with sirens to Coachella. And what am I doing? Sitting on a folding chair in an office above a parking garage with no windows and only one pathetic fan to hold the summer heat at bay. If I would've worked yesterday, I would've been set. Gunnar was working yesterday and he's part Jotun, so this place was probably cool as an alpine lake. Instead, I'm stuck with *Otto*.

"You know, in the good old days, if someone wanted to go on a Quest they had to wait for a mentor or a divine summons. The Oracle of Delphi used to be a real person, you know."

Having the same shift as Otto is *the worst*.

"These so-called Knights nowadays – most of them have never even *met* a king or queen, you know. It used to be that you had to distinguish yourself in service before you were knighted. You couldn't just...take a test and get a license."

Our boss leans over to me and whispers, "The only 'good' thing about the 'good old days' is that they're gone."

I grin.

I work for a company called Midnight Pumpkin. It's a corporation that hooks drivers up with Knights who need rides to wherever their Quest Request sends them. With hazard pay and tips, it's not bad money. There's also something to be said for being on the sidelines of history.

Of course, it's always just that: the sidelines. When I was a kid, I wanted to be a Knight. I pictured myself getting a Request on my phone from Delphi International and leaping into action. Those daydreams usually involved lots of epic swordfights and dragons. Instead, I'm the mouse-turned-coachman taking Snow White to slay the Jabberwocky. But, you know, I'm an adult now. It pays the bills.

Anyway, my "coach" is awesome. When I first got her, she was the same as all the other surplus police cruisers Midnight Pumpkin keeps on hand. Our boss is the best, though, and we're allowed to do whatever modifications we want. So now, KITTI is *cool* as nitrogen, if you catch my drift. All puns intended.

"Yo, I got something for you." Boss Man leans over me about two hours into Otto's latest rant and hands me a sticky note with two addresses on it. "A Knight needs a lift into a warzone and I know how much you love dodging missiles."

I raise an eyebrow at him. "Why are *you* taking calls? I thought menial jobs were below you."

"Yeah, well, the operators work in a soundproof room, so..." He tilts his head in the direction of Otto, who caught onto the fact that no one is listening and has dialed it back to grumbling under his breath.

"Understood." I take the sticky note between two fingers and make my escape.

"Have fun!" Boss Man calls. Then, as an afterthought, "Don't die!"

The Knight I'm picking up is waiting on the concrete steps in front of an underwhelmingly average brownstone. The only indicator that she's the one I'm here to pick up is the skintight, bulletproof mesh suit we still call "chainmail". It shines in the sun like metal would and is composed of interlocking patterns of material, but that's where the similarities end. She shoulders a backpack and heads towards me.

I park on the curb and roll down the passenger window. "Susanna?"

"That's me," she nods. Lifting her shoulder to indicate the backpack strap slung over it, she asks, "Can I put this in the backseat?"

"Go ahead." I thumb the unlock button.

Susanna and I have the same taste in music, so it takes her forever to decide which of my CD's to feed into KITTI's above average sound system. (Not to toot my own horn.) Once she does, we pass about an hour of the trip just vibing to the rhythm. I hum and tap the steering wheel to the music every now and then. For a while, I try to stop when I catch myself doing it. After all, I pride myself on service and professionalism and some people hate that kind of thing. Then Susanna starts drumming her fingers on her thighs and all bets are off.

I pull into a gas station at the hour and a half mark. Susanna raises an eyebrow at me.

"I need the bathroom," I say. "Feel free to grab some snacks from the store; my treat."

"Thanks, but I think I'll just hit the restroom, too."

Her definition of hitting the restroom is a lot different than mine. We enter our stalls at the same time, but she's practically washing her hands by the time I sit down. On my way out, I get a coffee and a bag of Skittles. There's a window next to the checkout counter and KITTI is right outside. I glance over as the machine processes my card and see Susanna flipping through my CD stash again.

I climb inside just as she feeds a new CD in and shake the Skittles in her direction. "Have some. They're lucky."

"How d'ya figure?"

"I used to eat them before I took a test," I say. "The only time I didn't, I totally bombed."

"That's pretty airtight logic." She reaches in and pulls out a few using her fingers like the claw in those machines with the stuffed animals and twenty-cent rubber duckies. She's still looking at me after she gets her Skittles. "What made you want to chauffer Knights around?"

"That's a good question." I tap my fingers on the steering wheel. "I don't really know. I mean, I was originally just doing this part-time while I was in college, but then I graduated and...nobody else wanted to hire me. I interviewed with all these organizations, but I kept getting passed up. Meanwhile, I was doing this and I felt like I was doing something that almost really mattered just by helping people who were doing things that mattered."

"You are doing something that matters," Susanna says.

I laugh. "No, I'm just the driver."

"We need people who do all kinds of things in order to complete the Quests," she says. "If everyone was a Knight, how would we get anywhere? Who would make the weapons? Who would feed us or give us a place to stay?"

"That's a good point," I concede, checking over my shoulder and gunning it to make it off the freeway entrance before a purple sedan.

"It's not just a good point, it's the truth." She can tell I'm not buying it and she's not about to let that slide. "Think about it; every job matters. If you took away even one occupation our world would be vastly different. In the end, everyone is essential."

"Huh." I think about it, like she said. I can't come up with a single occupation I could get rid of without altering our way of life. I wonder why I never realized that before. Even hereditary monarchs fulfill an important role by giving the ninety-nine percent someone to complain about.

As soon as the joke pops through my head, I feel the glare across the fifteen or so generations separating me from my sovereign ancestors. *Sorry,* I think, trying to send the message back along our bloodline like it's a temporal telegraph wire. I'm not sure if it works because for the rest of the ride whenever I catch my own eyes in the rearview mirror, I look annoyed.

We hit the edge of the city which is our destination around twilight. It looks like it was hit by a meteor shower. Some buildings are pocked with holes while others have tumbled into each other like dominoes. Some windows are lit up, but the flickering makes it clear the light is from fire, not lightbulbs. There's so much smoke in the air it looks like the city's shrouded in gray fog. Almost immediately after passing the population sign, there's a boom and a scream.

"Incoming," Susanna warns through her teeth.

I'm already swerving out of the way of the missile. It impacts behind us, the shockwave sending the car spinning. I don't fight it, using it instead to slingshot around and up the street.

"I hope you're buckled up," I grin.

Susanna has one hand on her gun, the other clenching the seat with white knuckles. "Are you sure? You can drop me off and escape."

I roll my eyes. "I do this for a living, and you think I've never been shot at before?"

The shockwave wasn't so bad the first time, but I'd rather not get caught in another. I make a quick turn down a side road, zig-zagging through the streets and back alleys with the pedal all the way to the floor. After a few missiles impact far enough behind us that we're clear of the blast, they get smart and start aiming at where we'll be.

I hear the screaming and see the missile on a collision course, so I slam on the brakes and wrench the wheel, spinning the car around. By the time the missile hits, we're gunning it in the opposite direction.

"Looks like there's a lot of debris in the road this way," Susanna says.

"Uh-huh."

I dodge into the other lane when I can. When the alley is too narrow, I lean the car over onto one set of tires in order to squeeze around the impact zones. At least some good is coming from everyone being forced to evacuate; I don't have to worry about other drivers in addition to a supervillain.

A moving target is remarkably hard to hit, even with a bird's eye view and missile launchers. On top of that, missiles take a while to reload. It's basically a race at this point; I'm trying to get out of range and they're trying to hit me before I do.

There aren't obvious turrets, so I figure they're hiding in one of the skyscrapers. It's smart because a less experienced driver might get closer by accident. But I'm pretty good at judging direction and distance, which means every missile gives me a better idea of where the shooters are. I have it narrowed down to one of the buildings by the time I pull out of the third alley. After that, it's just a matter of making trouble for whoever has to aim the things.

They're nice enough to send some cars after us, which I love now that I sprang for the bulletproof glass. Sending in ground troops can backfire pretty quickly, because you can't shoot missiles when your own guys are right there. Of course, if a guy is leaning out one of the windows with a grenade launcher, missiles aren't necessary. Which they accounted for, apparently. I don't feel bad when I dodge out of the way and the grenade hits the car behind me. He should've taken his cues from the missile squad and kept track of his fellow minions.

I'd love to say I picked up the maneuvers I use in car chases from my harrowing adventures, but the truth is most of the stuff is based off the bumper car obsession I had back in middle school. I nail one car next to the back tire, causing it to spin out into one of it's buddies. Then it's just me and the car in front, with the *dummkopf* who accidentally shot his own people.

I floor it, accelerating towards him. The driver is apparently more experienced than the shooter and hits the brakes, hoping I'll knock out my engine on his fender. I yank the wheel, which sends me spinning around to face the opposite direction. I shift into reverse and speed by the car backwards. The expressions of drivers when you shoot by them like that is just free serotonin.

I keep driving in reverse until I get to an intersection, then I shift into drive. As I do, I realize I've been blessed with a long, straight road that's remained remarkably untouched. Not to mention I'm out of missile range, which means the last thing I have to do is outrun this joker. I press a button under the dash, and then we're *flying*. Susanna and I slam back into our seats with the force of it. It's all I can do to keep my hands on the wheel. Our pursuer never had a chance.

As soon as we've officially lost them — okay, maybe I indulged myself a little longer than I needed to — I slow down and try to reorient myself. The maps app on my phone is out of the question given the sheer quantity of supervillains who either are or employ hackers, so I had to print out the directions before I left work. To be safe, I also pinpointed the location on a map and studied it. I don't have a photographic memory, but I have an idea of which direction I need to go. Besides, if we get lost and drive around randomly, we'll be less likely to lead anyone to the base.

"You alright?" I ask Susanna.

She's pale. "I'm glad I only had those Skittles during our break."

I laugh.

"That," she takes a deep breath, "was incredible."

I laugh harder. "You sound like you mean it's incredible that we're still alive."

"Well, I was talking about your driving." She sucks in some more air. "But that too, yes." She looks at me out of the corner of her eye and smiles. "I can't believe you think what you're doing is unimportant."

It's nice of her to say, but I'm not sure I believe her. After all, I'm not doing something anyone else couldn't do. I'm just driving my car. Lots of people drive their cars every day. There are plenty more taxi drivers where I came from, too. I'm just a normal person.

Susanna's fellow Knights (Company?) are taking shelter in an apartment building surrounded on all sides by identical apartment buildings. Even knowing the address, I'm not sure I'd be able to identify the right one if a Knight wasn't leaning against the wall. He walks out into the middle of the street as I approach, then beckons me into an alley like a marshaller directing a plane on a runway.

"Alright." I sigh, putting the car in park and relaxing. "Good luck with everything, and, uh, thank you for choosing Midnight Pumpkin. Keep us in mind for—"

"You're not leaving right now, are you?" Susanna asks.

I raise an eyebrow. "I'm not sure how many of the sights are still there for the seeing."

"You can't just go *back*, it's *dangerous*."

I close my eyes and hope she can't see them rolling under my eyelids. "I'll be fine. They probably won't expect me to leave immediately, so they might not even see me on the way out."

"Forgive me if 'probably' and 'might' don't make me feel better."

"You're forgiven."

She glances over my shoulder at her friend. "Just come in for a minute. Rest."

The other Knight knocks on my window. "Everything okay?" He asks.

I sigh heavily. "Fine. I have to use the bathroom anyway."

*

How did I let them talk me into this?

Susanna recruited a bunch of the others while I was in the bathroom, the traitor. They ganged up on me and convinced me to stick around until they're done toppling the invaders. I can hold my own okay against one hero complex, but six of them overpowered me. So, I'm stuck here for the time being. Of course, if it takes them more than two days to get rid of these guys, I'll have to make a run for it. I have my rent to think about.

The apartment the Knights have chosen is a pretty nice place considering someone's been razing the city for two days now. If I ever wondered what the aftermath of a giant picking up a building and shaking it would be, I don't have to anymore. Anything that wasn't bolted down has been tossed around, fragile things shattering and sturdy things rolling under larger things like they're trying to hide. I bet the furniture was tipped over when they first found the place, but most of it is upright now. Knights can't help themselves from trying to fix things.

Susanna, as it turns out, has the ability to become invisible. She's the one who's going to sneak some of the others into the invaders' base of operations while the rest stage a diversion. Even now, hours later, I swell with pride to know that such a valuable member of the team rode in *my* car.

This afternoon, I actually got to watch her and the other Knights train. They're incredible. I can't imagine the work and energy that went into becoming so skilled. I couldn't do that. I'm not as disciplined.

They offered me a bed, but I took the couch. There are too many people here for everyone to have a nice place to sleep, even when they take turns standing guard. I'm not about to cheat someone out of a bed on the night before a big battle. I wanted to take the floor, but they all looked offended when I suggested it.

Given their generosity, I feel bad that I don't sleep well in places other than my apartment and my parents' house. I toss and turn for a few hours, wrestling with sleep. At three in the morning, I call a time out and get up for a drink of water.

Susanna's on watch, staked out by the window across the room. Fortunately, the living room is the only one in the apartment with a window *and* a hall entrance. Because it's the only spot anyone could get in or out, only one person needs to be on watch at a time, which means everyone gets to sleep longer. If they can, that is. When I get up, Susanna glances in my direction and smiles. I wave.

A boy around my age is in the kitchen already, sitting at the table as one leg does a fantastic impersonation of a jackhammer. He's resting his chin on one hand and staring in the direction of a pastoral painting, though he seems to be looking straight through it. His dark auburn bangs hang in front of his eyes, but he doesn't move to brush them away. Because I watched him spar with the others, I know that he doesn't have x-ray vision or anything. It's possible he just didn't mention it, but it wouldn't go with the rest of his schtick; he can give substance to shadows and create constructs out of them. So, this is likely a normal, pedestrian case of spacing out.

"Hey." I forget about the water for a second and sit down across from him.

When he snaps his head up and I realize I underestimated how out of it he was.

"Sorry," I say. "I didn't mean to startle you."

"No. You didn't. I'm fine." His words are clipped and quick, like he's trying to catch them between his teeth.

"What's going on?" I ask.

He laughs almost hysterically. Normally, that would be a red flag, but on a Quest it's the sanest kind of laugh you can make. "Look around! These people conquered *the whole city*. The *government* can't even stop them! That's why there was a Request, you know. Because the army *failed*. Did you know that?"

"I had a hunch," I say.

"Well, it was spot on."

I snort a laugh. "That's so British."

He frowns. "I'm trying to have a crisis here, and you're kind of ruining it."

"That was the intention." I swing my legs. "Look, uh...what's your name again?"

"Luke."

"That is a fantastic Questing name," I tell him, winking. "Look, Luke; you're a Knight. This is what you're passionate about. And yeah, it's dangerous, but that's part of what makes it fun, right? And it's part of why no one else can do what you do. You Knights are dedicated, smart, skilled, and brave. That's just what you are. So, you don't have to worry about messing up or chickening out or whatever, because you're already the best person for the job. If *you* can't do it, maybe it wasn't meant to be done."

He squints at me. "Who are you, again?"

Okay, he's noticed one of these things is not like the others. That's a good sign. It means his head is back in the vicinity of the game. "I'm Lila," I say. "I'm from Midnight Pumpkin."

"You should think about a career in motivational speaking."

"I shall."

"That's so British," he says. It's a weak attempt, but progress is progress.

I pat his shoulder. "Now go get some sleep. You can take the couch; I'm not going to be able to sleep anyway. I can never sleep in a strange place."

"I can't—"

"You can and you will," I tell him. "Just like on this Quest."

He smiles.

~

The next time I see Luke, another Knight is carrying him into the apartment building. Luke is bleeding hard from his gut. I suddenly feel like I'm about to cough up my heart. *I talked him into this.*

"Hey! Susanna said you can get us out of the city," The other Knight says. She's pressing what I assume is her jacket against Luke's wound. Her eyes are as wide as her pupils are shrunken, hands dyed red and sticky from blood that's already soaked through the fabric.

"Yeah, I can." I grab my keys and head for the window.

When I parked in the alley earlier, I noticed that we were close to the fire escape. Always a good thing if we need to make a quick exit. The window is jammed, refusing to move when I yank at it. Checking to make sure it's unlocked, I try a few more times before giving up.

I growl and throw a hand out behind me. "Back up!"

Pulling the hem of my shirt up, I slide my pistol from its holster. It's small enough to fit comfortably in my hand, and the grip is decorated with engraved roses. When I'm anxious, I use it as a potentially deadly worry stone.

Aiming at the corners, I squeeze off four shots. Some glass is still caught in the frame, but the pressure has let up enough that I can actually open it now. I crawl out onto the fire escape and holster the gun, then turn around to help the other Knight slide Luke through the window.

He still has baby-round cheeks, but he weighs what a guy who fights crime for a living should; heavy with muscle and courage. Glass crunches under my sneakers as we shuffle around. The other Knight is seriously jacked, which is probably one of the reasons she's the one who carried Luke back here. I have to climb up on the edge of the landing's railing so the three of us can fit on the platform. I lean back against the ladder and curl one ankle around one of the posts, balancing there until the Knight pulls Luke back into her arms. Once I'm sure she's got him, I let go with my ankle and drop off the fire escape, grabbing the side of the ladder and swinging myself onto it as I fall.

I'm too busy climbing towards my car and spamming the unlock button on my fob to see how the Knight manages to get Luke and herself down. She slides into the backseat almost as soon as I turn the key, so I assume she used her powers. I know I saw her use them yesterday, but I can't remember what they are for the life of me.

I buckle up and glance in the rearview mirror. "You're going to want to hold on."

Tentacles sprout from her fingers. Three of them wind themselves around Luke, keeping him still and putting pressure on his wound. The other seven brace against the sides of the car.

I nod, impressed. "That'll do it."

I ease us slowly to the end of the alley. I don't want to shake Luke around in this state, and if we can escape without attracting attention that would be perfect. Unfortunately, as soon as I pull onto the street, headlights flash on from all sides like they're trying to blind me. I glower. This isn't just a job anymore; I feel responsible for Luke. It's personal.

Those minions should've stayed out of my way.

*

"I got us out of the city alright. The nearest hospital was still pretty far away, so..." I shrug at my cellmate. "I think I broke, like, twenty different traffic laws. Also the cops were chasing me for the last thirty miles or so."

"That's rad," she says in awe. She's a scrawny thing in chains and heavy makeup. Earlier, she told me she got collared for pick-pocketing. I'm not surprised. Her outfit doesn't exactly blend in with the crowd.

"Thanks."

"What happened to Luke?"

I smile. "He's going to be alright. The other Knight left a mes-sage for me with my boss, and he told me all about it when I called."

"Cool." She leans back against the cement wall, smiling with satisfaction. I couldn't see how young she was when she was posturing and all, but now it hits me in the gut. She can't be over twenty. Catching me watching her, she asks, "Shouldn't they just let you out? Because you were helping the Knights?"

"The rules are complicated." I shrug. "It's fine, though. My boss will get the charges waived; he always does."

"He sounds nice," she says. "I wish I had a boss like that."

"Oh yeah?" I link my arms behind my head and look up at the ceiling casually. "How's your driving?"

Making plans to get the girl – Naomi – a job with Midnight Pumpkin keeps us busy for a little while, but soon enough our conversation fades. Naomi turns her attention to scratching something on the wall and I grab a magazine left for us by one of the cops. It's something about housekeeping and decorating, so it might as well be written in French for all the sense it makes to me. I start wondering if I'll get fined for making a paper airplane out of one of the pages.

The door at the end of the hall opens and I wonder if one of the cops is telepathic and picked up on my vandalistic intent. I put the magazine down on my chest and look through the bars. I'm pretty sure it's someone here to talk to one of the other inmates, so it takes me a minute to recognize the woman trailing behind the cop.

I sit up abruptly. "Susanna?"

As soon as she catches sight of me, she smiles. "Lila, hey!"

"How did it go? Is everyone alright?" I stand up and walk over to the bars, looking her over. She must have just come from the fight; her hair is mussed, uniform torn in places, and there's streaks of dirt and grime all over her.

"We did it!" She smiles, exhausted but happy. "I managed to shut everything down from inside, and after that it was just a straight brawl. It took forever, but we made it."

The cop twists a key in the lock and swings open my cell door. I step out cautiously, not totally sure what he expects me to do. He doesn't seem upset and swings the door shut behind me. I wave at Naomi before following Susanna back down the hall, the cop at my back.

"It's so nice of you to come visit me," I say. "Really, you should go home first. Get some rest and come back later."

She looks over her shoulder. "I'm not here to *visit*."

"What?"

"The lady paid your bail," the cop chimes in. "You're free to go."

"What?!"

Susanna holds the door open for me, but I don't walk through.

"You don't have to do that," I tell her. "My boss will get me out, you shouldn't waste your money—"

"It's not a *waste*!" She snaps.

I flinch backwards, blinking. I didn't think she had it in her to be intimidating, but this day is just full of surprises.

Her expression softens. "You saved Luke's life. It's the least we can do."

"I think that was the doctors, actually," I correct her. "Also, 'we'?"

"The whole team pitched in. We wanted you to join us in celebrating, and when we found out where you were we had to get you out."

"Susanna, I can't accept this."

"Your selflessness is wonderful, really, but I'm starving and I really want to get out of here." Sighing, she gets behind me and propels me out of the station.

I don't have the heart to turn her down. It's such a sweet gesture, and I'd hate to insult the Knights right after they saved an entire city. So, I let it happen while making a mental note to talk to the

Boss Man about reimbursing them later. I mean, I was just doing my job. They're the heroes, after all. I'm just the driver.

LOVE IS A MYTH

For Mom

Seaside villages are known for a few things; great local seafood, sailing, and cryptids. This particular village was no exception; Arnold's Diner had the best clam chowder in the tristate area, the marina was state of the art, and the local cryptid lived in the lighthouse.

Summer was coming to an end, the wind off the water growing chillier and sharper as the hemisphere shifted away from the sun. Arnold's still had their outside tables set up, hoping to get a few more weeks of tourists before battening down the hatches for the colder months. It was a good move, as it turned out, because for the past week unseasonal warmth had beaten back the encroaching autumn.

As the sun blazed down on the village, two brothers scooted their chairs around the table so the light didn't sear into their corneas. Nick and Jake were Irish twins and looked identical despite the miniscule age difference. Oddly enough, they were ethnically Irish, too, and looked the part. Both had green eyes and hair so red anyone who hadn't known them as kids would swear it came out of a bottle. Their faces were galaxies of freckles that had darkened with the rest of their skin in the summer sun.

"Dude," Jake said, shaking his brother's shoulder.

Nick was playing a game on his phone and almost missed a jump. He elbowed his older brother, annoyed. Jake would not be deterred, shaking him again.

"Nick! Heads up!"

Nick aimed for his face that time, but Jake dodged. The younger boy's phone slipped from his hand and fell to the dirt. At the tell-tale jingle of a failed level, he spun to unleash the full force of his wrath. Jake pushed his head to the side.

"Look! She's here!"

Nick straightened up immediately and hoped she hadn't seen them yet. It's common knowledge that cryptids will disappear if they catch anyone watching them. He stuck the toe of his sneaker under his phone and kicked it up, catching it and holding it in front of his face so he could stare without being obvious.

Almost everyone was dressed in shorts and t-shirts to keep from getting heat stroke, so she would've stood out due to her outfit choice alone. She wore her signature coat; a sleek, knee-length silver gray which looked like leather but – they had it on good authority – was actually coated in velvety fur. She always wore it, regardless of weather or occasion.

Under the coat, her skin was white. Not Caucasian; white. Like paper or a corpse. Her hair was the same non-color and her eyes were bright red. Alone, she looked pale and sick. Next to her French/Maliseet family, she looked like someone had drained her insides out along with all the pigment in her body.

Jake and Nick knew what an albino was. If she was just albino, she might not have caught their attention like she had. But oh, there was so much more.

When they were in kindergarten, she'd been in their class for half a year. Her brothers were in higher grades, her sister already in middle school. One day, she just...stopped going. She never set foot in a public school again. Her siblings, however, went on to become athletes, student council members, and theatre stars. Their little sister didn't come to a single performance and only attended a handful of outdoor games. When she did show up, she wore thick black sunglasses even after the sun set.

Jake and Nick had grown up on Celtic folklore and cryptid hunter YouTube channels, so they were pretty sure they knew what was going on. A girl who looked human yet was uncomfortable around humans, always came from the direction of the sea, and obsessively refused to be parted with her fur coat? Clearly, the lighthouse operators had discovered a baby selkie during a storm and decided to raise her as their own. Of course they hadn't hidden her coat; it was an adoption, not a kidnapping. And she loved them, too, so instead of vanishing into the ocean when she felt its call, she would transform into her seal body for a few days before returning to her human family. Honestly, they were almost too obvious about it.

Selkie came into town occasionally, but only visited booths or businesses that allowed walk-ups at their drive thru windows. Jake was convinced it was part of her nature; the aversion to being away from the sea.

"The Earth is one big electromagnetic neutralizer, right?" he'd explained to Nick. "As long as she's in contact with the ground, she's technically connected to the ocean."

"I don't know how," Nick had replied slowly, "but I understood the statement and not your explanation of it."

That day, Selkie was buying strawberries from the back of a pickup truck with rust flaking off the sides. The proprietor was a woman who looked even smaller than she already was next to the mechanical monster. Selkie said something, and after a moment of laughter they exchanged red berries for green paper. Selkie's laugh was throaty, similar to barking. Nick liked it.

"Where's she going now?" He hissed at his brother. "She can't be going back already, can she?"

"How should I know?" Jake whispered back. Then, "Duck!"

The two of them hunched over, feigning intense interest in their blank screens. It was a truly pathetic display of acting, but Selkie's gaze swept over them and continued on across the road. She checked one more time before jogging through the crosswalk.

"Get the check," Nick said. "I'm going in."

Before his brother could argue, he got up and strode across the street with exaggerated casualness. He had to stretch his stride to keep up. Selkie had short legs, but they moved twice as fast as a normal person's. Also, she had a head start. He did his best not to look like he was following her, making a show of looking at his phone every now and then and "hesitating" at intersections. He'd seen enough crime shows to know not to be obvious about tailing a mark.

They ended up at the library; a large, flat building made of bricks and the sum total of human knowledge. The American flag fluttered majestically in the wind from a fifty-foot silver pole. Someone was coming through the revolving doors when Selkie got to them, but she didn't wait for them to exit. She kept walking, passing effortlessly through. Nick wondered if she was inhumanly self-confident or if she just went to the library enough that she had it down to a science. *He* had to wait until he was the only one using the doors before he could enter.

The city library had been standing since the eighteen-hundreds and hadn't gone through many updates since. Every Wednesday, they turned off the electricity and used the old oil lamps that still hung from the walls. It gave off an air of mystery and magic, so Nick wasn't surprised to see Selkie visiting.

It took him maybe three minutes to catch up with her inside the building, but she was already heading back towards the front desk. That was a problem. How was he supposed to look inconspicuous if he left immediately after her without even looking around? Selkie pushed the book towards the librarian and dug around in her pockets for her library card.

Nick made a beeline for a display on a wooden table near the entrance. The covers were evenly split between black-and-white photographs of famous activists and colorful illustrations with oil pastel vibes. Nick picked up a biography of Nelsen Mandela and flipped it over. He couldn't concentrate on the words, too busy keeping his peripheral on Selkie.

She started for the door, and he put the book down. Leaning back, he put his hands in his pockets and studied the banner over the table with barely believable faux interest. He read it five times in the flickering lamplight before the words actually made sense. "August: International Peace Month."

Nick raked his eyes over the books on display one more time for good measure, then pivoted and headed back out. In front of the library, he looked around like the Terminator trying to reestablish a visual link to Sarah Connor. His phone rang and he picked up reluctantly.

"Hey," he said.

"Where are you guys?" Jake asked. *"Please tell me you didn't lose her."*

Nick rocked back on his heels. "Okay."

Jake groaned. *"Next time, you pay for the meal and I'll follow the cryptid, okay?"*

Their conversation continued as they headed towards each other, meeting up at a gas station halfway. The road was curved, lined on both sides by thick clusters of trees. This meant they weren't able to see Selkie emerging from the library, wiping her hands on her jeans and cursing internally at whoever decided an air dryer that moved at a snail's pace was a good replacement for a roll of paper towels.

She headed back the way she'd come. When she passed the gas station, Jake and Nick were inside trying to figure out if they wanted ice cream or nachos. Neither of them looked up from the snacks. Neither of them saw her cross the street and keep walking straight out of town.

{ (o.o) }

The anxiety the oncoming school year induced was worse than usual. Jake and Nick, eighteen and seventeen-and-a-half respectively, were going to be seniors. It was their last summer as high schoolers. They wanted – *needed* – to make the most of it.

When Nick had turned thirteen, the boys had decided to share a room. They'd shoved the mess in Jake's room into a big pile of disaster, somehow managed to maneuver Nick's bed into the empty space, and turned Nick's old room into a clubhouse. They'd used their birthday money to buy bean bag chairs, covered the windows with cardboard scavenged from the recycling bin, and strung old Christmas lights along the walls. Over the years, it had become a pretty sweet hangout. They'd gotten a secondhand TV, convinced their cousins to give them an old game system, brought in some lava lamps, and even managed to get a mini fridge.

Nick was lying on his stomach, legs trailing of the bag of the bean bag. He snapped a little blue guy's neck in Among Us, then glanced up at the TV. They'd pulled up *MythBusters* on Hulu and were halfway through the ninth season. Jake had on headphones with a microphone curled in front of his face. He was also multi-tasking; watching the show and playing a sci-fi MMORPG.

"You know what would be sick?" He asked.

"What?" Nick replied at the same time as a few of Jake's online teammates.

He made a face and leaned into the mike. "No, no, not you guys. Sorry." He muted himself and pulled his headphones down around his neck. "Okay. Picture a speedboat, but with a tent or something set up in the back...maybe like one of those blinds people use for hunting. It would be like a houseboat, but really fast."

Nick nodded thoughtfully and shanked a pink player in the back. "We could do, like, a water version of the Great Lakes Circuit. And if we brought a portable generator, we could even hook it up with Wi-Fi."

"I don't think Mom and Dad would let us borrow the Wi-Fi that long."

"Yeah, but we could get our own. Maybe with one of those prepay plans? We could just cancel after the trip." Nick smirked at the chat on his phone. Someone had found the body. *Purple sus,* he typed. *Saw them with Pink.*

Lies! Purple protested.

Purple said vote pink last round, said Orange.

Nick did his best evil laugh.

"What are you doing?" Jake asked.

"Causing chaos. As I was born to do." Nick flipped over on his back and looked up at his brother. "When are we going to do the trip, though? We'd have to leave, like, immediately."

"Also, we're flat broke."

"And that."

"I was thinking of waiting until next summer," Jake said. "We could use the money we get from graduation and—" An alien zombie jumped out in front of his group. He swore and started spamming buttons.

Nick ended up getting flushed out of the airlock before the zombie battle was even halfway over. He put his phone on his chest and waited. In the book *Pictures in the Cave*, George MacKay Brown describes selkies as having white skin. Maybe Lighthouse Selkie wasn't an albino after all. Or maybe *all* selkies were albinos. It would make sense, seeing as the legends usually described them shedding their sealskins at night. That would be easier on eyes without melanin.

Nick wondered if selkies liked boat rides. They could swim better than humans, but they couldn't be faster than speedboats. It might be like a roller coaster for her.

"Anyway, like I was saying…" Jake slid down his beanbag, stretching his leg until he was able to just barely kick his brother in the head.

Nick grunted and turned, glaring at him.

Jake smirked. "Anyway, like I was saying; we'll probably get a lot of money for graduation. I heard Ted Baxter's sister got over a thousand dollars."

"What? Seriously?" Nick frowned. "Is he the Ted with a million aunts and uncles though?"

"No, that's Ted Beaner. Both of Baxter's parents come from standard, two-point-five child families."

"Really?" Nick looked ecstatic, then frowned. "But what if they do that thing where they give us each half the amount they'd usually give? Because there are two of us."

"Huh. Didn't think about that." Jake unmuted himself. "We should definitely not trust this guy...Yeah, I know, but...Okay, look; I think..." He glanced at Nick and rolled his eyes dramatically. "Okay, yeah, whatever. But *when* we die, I'm going to complain about it for the rest of the campaign." He muted himself again. "We could hunt cryptids as we go."

"That would be awesome!" Nick grinned. "We can study Native American legends during the school year, and by the time we go on the trip we'll be experts."

"Right, that's what I was thinking, too." Jake nodded. "Maybe check out the other big ethnic groups around the lake. You never know if someone brought something with them from the Old World."

The door opened, sending light from the hallway spilling into the comfortable dimness of the clubhouse. It was bright enough by comparison to force Jake to squint, blinking, as he waited for the new arrival to look like more than a silhouette.

Nick was off to the side and the light didn't completely blind him, so he recognized her right away. She was average height with above-average muscle tone, cassiterite-brown skin, and a light chestnut afro.

"Hi, Cam!" He waved. "You here for your boyfriend?"

"Nah, I'm here for your mom's brownies. Jake's just a fringe benefit." Latisha Cameron popped the last corner of a brownie in her mouth and licked her fingers.

"I'd be offended, but honestly I can't blame you." Jake set his laptop aside and stood up, stretching. He tossed a wave in Nick's direction. "Don't get eaten or something before I get back, okay?"

Nick rolled his eyes. "Of course not. I'd only do something that might get me eaten if you were with me."

"Oh yeah?" Jake puffed out his chest. "Need your big brother's protection?"

"I need a diversion so I can escape."

{ (o.o) }

It was still relatively early for a summer night, the sun just starting to kiss the horizon. The undersides of the clouds were airbrushed orange and pink, which would get more vivid as the sun sank lower. Nick left after dinner for a walk, intending to head for the beach to see if anything interesting had washed up in the tide. Plans change, especially when one catches sight of the illusive selkie.

She was curled up in the lower branches of a tree reading a book. Despite her massive sunglasses, Nick could see the way her brow wrinkled in concentration. She was holding a pen between her fingers like a cigarette. As he watched, she flipped the book on its side and jotted something in the margin.

He hid behind a different tree and considered his options. He could walk past her casually, which might get him a peek at the title. Then what? Walking back and forth in front of her would be suspicious. From what he'd read, selkies were relatively harmless as supernatural creatures went, but she could still spook.

He could stay hidden until she left, then follow her. The only other option he could think of was heading for the road up to the lighthouse and waiting. Still, if she *was* a selkie she might not even use the road. It might be easier for her to slip into her sealskin behind the changing house on the beach and swim the rest of the way.

He turned and stood on his toes to peer through the gap created when the tree's trunk split in two. She flipped a page and shifted her grip, one hand hunting behind her as she read. She pulled a green shake of some kind from the branches. A smoothie? Were seals herbivores? Nick slid his phone out of his pocket and typed quickly in the search bar, careful not to look away from her for too long. Who knew how she'd pulled the disappearing trick earlier?

All seals are carnivores, the internet informed him.

Nick frowned, narrowing his eyes at the cup. Maybe selkies were omnivores, like humans.

After slurping up the remaining drops, she put the cup between her knees and shoved the book and pen into an inside pocket of her coat. Dropping nimbly to the ground, she started down the sidewalk, tossing the cup in a trash can along the way.

Thankfully, she was headed away from Nick. He wanted her to get enough of a head start that she wouldn't notice him, but he also didn't want to lose her again. He started after her, making sure his eyes were on the sidewalk near her shoes so she wouldn't feel his gaze on her back. They headed vaguely in the direction of the lighthouse, but not towards the road Nick would've taken.

He congratulated himself on not trying to wait for her there. They weren't heading towards the beach, either, which was strange. It didn't click until he could see the forest in the distance.

Nick had driven by the hiking trail a million times and walked it more often than he could remember. It curled through the woods like a snake, and just before it looped back towards town there was a part where the lighthouse was clearly visible through the trees. It made a lot of sense that Selkie would cut through the forest from the trail instead of going the long way around by road or water.

Luckily for Nick, there were still a few hikers and bikers, probably soaking up the last of the summer for all it was worth. Still, it wasn't like they were following the leader. He hated to do it, but he fell back so Selkie wouldn't catch on. He did his best to stay at least one bend behind her, so for the most part it was just him and the woods.

Night fell faster under leaves that blocked the sun. He focused on the path in front of him, squinting against shadows that hid rocks and roots. It wasn't something he noticed happening, but there was a big difference between the visibility at the beginning of the hike and that of when he reached the loop parallel to the lighthouse. He hadn't considered what he'd do when he got there, so focused on not tripping he almost kept walking down the trail. Just as he was about to bypass the lighthouse entirely, the wind shifted. A chill blew directly into his face.

He looked up, scanning what he could of the sky through the trees. Dark clouds spread across the horizon opposite the sunset. How long had they been there? He took out his phone and checked the time. If he wanted to make it home before the storm hit – or worse; his parents got worried – he'd have to start back soon.

As he debated, he flicked on his flashlight and panned the beam along the tree line. If he hadn't been looking for it, he would've assumed the flattened leaves and broken branches indicated a deer trail. But there was no other way to get off at this stop, unless selkies could phase through solid objects. Staring at the path, he sighed. He threw one last backwards glance at the gathering storm – was it closer already? – and forged ahead.

Once the shadows had a foothold in the forest, they spread like weeds. He tried to stay on the path, but the problem with a deer trail – or, in this case, a selkie trail – is that it's very easy to miss a turn and head off in another direction. Inevitably, he got lost. He did his best to angle himself towards the lighthouse whenever he caught sight of it. They hadn't turned it on for some reason, but the dying sunlight reflected off the glass occasionally. Nick kept his eyes on it until it was swallowed, over and over, by the forest.

I am a moth and this is my flame, he thought, smirking. *Except I'm not going to get fried by it.*

That was the last coherent thought he had before the ground dropped out from under him. There was a moment of wordless panic as he fell. He didn't remember hitting the ground.

{ (o.o) }

Rain battered the windows, thunder rumbling like an engine in the sky. Nick woke up sore in a room that smelled like seawater and fire. He was lying on something soft enough to be almost soothing against his aching body, covered by a heavy blanket that gave off a not-quite leathery smell. Everything hurt, like he'd been tenderized with a sledgehammer.

He opened his eyes slowly. The ceiling was composed of wooden boards, but the walls were stone. Not the fakey aesthetic that rich people liked, either; these were real stones stacked on top of each other, misshapen and uneven, gaps filled in with cement. About a yard away from where he lay was a fireplace, also made of stone.

He was lying on a couch decked out with a relatively new slipcover, but he'd bet money the couch itself was older than he was. He started to sit up, hissing in pain, and noticed someone near the fireplace. He froze.

The selkie was cross-legged on a carpet holding the same book and pen she had earlier. Nick felt his gut twisting. This was much more intimate than before – there was something about the storm outside and the dancing flames on the walls that bound them together in that moment. On top of that, she was barefoot, purple toenails glittering in the firelight. And she didn't have her coat on. Without it, she looked unbalanced. Definitely more proportional, her narrow shoulders and slim torso now matching her skinny legs, but he was used to her being top heavy with the fur. She looked like a different person without it. She looked...real.

Glancing over at the sound, her eyes widened. "Oh, you're awake. Good. I was getting worried you were in a coma or something."

"How—" The word stole the last of the moisture from his mouth and he coughed.

Selkie pointed behind him. "There's some water there. I don't know if it's warm now...I can get you more."

Nick twisted slowly, wincing, and grabbed the glass from the smooth wooden table next to him. He chugged the whole thing and set it down, then leaned back against the arm of the couch.

"Careful, you're pretty banged up," she warned.

"Mmph," he replied intelligently.

She got up and straightened his pillow so he could sit easier.

"Thanks. What happened?" he asked.

"I was walking in the woods when I heard a crash. I went to check it out and found you at the bottom of this little hill. You were unconscious and I couldn't carry you, so I ran and got my four-wheeler. I was going to try and take you to the hospital, but the storm hit and I figured this would be better." As she explained, she tilted back and forth in time to the rise and fall of her voice.

"Oh." There was something he was supposed to say in this situation. "Thank you." Nailed it.

Selkie gave him a small smile and nodded. "I'm just glad I heard you, otherwise you might still be out there."

"Yeah...that was...lucky..." It probably wasn't the best time to mention he'd been following her. He cleared his throat. "So, this is the lighthouse, huh? I always wanted to see it from the inside."

She looked around as if to see it from his point of view. "What do you think?"

"It's cool," he said. "I like the retro look."

She smirked. "Yeah, it works for us."

Which reminded him. "Where is everyone? Don't your parents and siblings live here, too?"

Her whole face drooped. "The twins are moving into their dorm, so Dominique and our parents went to help them."

"You...didn't want to go?" He asked carefully.

"I couldn't." She crossed her arms and looked away. "Their college has fluorescent lighting and screens everywhere... I get seizures from that kind of thing."

"Wow, I'm sorry." No wonder the room was lit by a fireplace and oil lamps. No wonder there was no TV in sight.

Selkie shrugged. "It's fine. I'm used to it. Speaking of which..." She got up and grabbed a beanie from a table on the other side of the room, then handed it to him.

Nick opened the hat. Inside was his phone – a little more cracked than it had been, but... He thumbed the power button reflexively. Selkie spun around quickly, hands flying to her face as the screen lit up beneath new spidery cracks.

"Oh shi—shoot! Sorry!" Nick shoved the phone under the blanket. Maybe he really *did* have a concussion, because once he really looked at the blanket his train of thought switched tracks instantly. "What is this, a bear skin?"

"Puma, actually. Can I turn around now?"

"Yeah! Sorry. Again."

"It's fine." She half-turned, then hesitated. "I should probably leave so you can call Jake or something."

"I guess – wait, how do you know Jake?"

She raised an eyebrow. "Nick, we ate lunch together every day for the only year I was in public school."

"Um. Right." He felt really guilty all of a sudden for just calling her by her species. "Of course. I remember, uh—"

"Mireille," she supplied.

"What?"

"My name is Mireille. In case you forgot."

"Meer-eye-yay," he attempted to mimic her.

"Mireille."

"Meer-eye-yeah." The sounds dropped, awkward and clumsy, like rocks from his tongue.

"It's French. Look." She grabbed a paperback from the mantle above the fireplace. Flipping the cover open, she pointed to the inscription on the title page.

To my dear Mireille

Happy Birthday!

Love, Papa

"Meer-ee-elle."

"Close enough." She smirked and shut the book, tossing it on a chair. "Anyway, I'll be in the kitchen if you need anything." She waved over her shoulder as she left.

Nick stared after her for an awkwardly long time before his brain finally caught up and he remembered what he was supposed to be doing. He opened his phone and called Jake.

Who picked up on the first ring. *"Nick?! Dude are you okay?! Where are you?!"*

"I'm fine!" He held up a hand as if to ward off Jake's questions, and the motion sent a lightning bolt of pain down his back. "Well – kind of. I fell off a cliff."

"You WHAT?!"

"Chill, it was a little cliff. Anyway, so I was unconscious—"

"What?!"

"—and Mireille found me and brought me back to her place—"

"Wait, who?"

Nick felt marginally better that he wasn't the only one who'd forgotten her name, but also a lot of second-hand guilt on top of the guilt he already had. So, one step forward and five steps back. "You know, the...the..." He couldn't exactly let on what they knew when she might be listening. "...The girl who lives in the lighthouse."

"You're with the selkie?!" Jake practically shouted.

"ANYWAY," Nick said loudly, "Just...I'm fine right now, okay? You can come get me, but..."

He frowned and glanced out the window. It hadn't seemed important enough to register with everything else that was going on, but now he could see it was pitch black outside. Would the headlights trigger Mireille's seizures? A crack of thunder shook the building, and he flinched.

"Is it even safe to be driving in this?" He wondered.

"Not according to the weather people."

A methodic clicking came across the line. Nick frowned, trying to place it. Then, "Wait, and you're driving anyway?!"

"No duh, Descartes."

Suddenly, the howling wind sounded a lot more menacing. "What – why?!" He knew, though.

"I've been looking for you, idiot!" Jake confirmed. *"Mom, Dad, Cam, and I have been over every inch of the city twice."*

"You have to get home!" Nick's grip tightened on the phone. "If it's not safe—"

"Nick, buddy," Jake's tone softened. *"We're worried about you right now. How bad are you hurt? Do you need to get to the hospital? Cam's dad has a truck that could make it up the road even if it's washed out."*

"I'm fine," Nick said. "I'm just resting now, I can wait."

"Are you actually, or are you just saying that because you're worried about us?"

"I'm actually fine."

"Would you tell me if you weren't?"

"I mean, probably not. But if it was bad I'd sound delirious or incoherent or something, right? Probably wouldn't even be using words like 'delirious' or 'incoherent'."

"I guess."

"Just get home, okay? Call the others. You can come get me as soon as the storm stops."

"Alright. But I'm calling you back every few hours to make sure you're not dead."

"Sounds like a plan. Text me when you get home so I know you're safe."

"Of course."

"Alright." Nick didn't want to hang up, gripped with an irrational fear that something bad would happen as soon as he couldn't hear Jake anymore. But the others wouldn't get the all-clear until he did. "Love you. Be safe."

"Love you too. Don't touch any runes."

"No promises."

Lightning flashed across the sky, and he heard a yelp followed by something shattering in the kitchen. His chest tightened. He stabbed at the screen and tossed the phone down, not checking to see if he'd hit the right button.

The door slammed against the wall as he shoved it open, looking wildly around the room. Unhelpfully, the room kept moving without him. He realized balance was no longer an option at the same time he admitted to himself it was possible Mireille was right about the concussion thing. As he fell, he tried to catch himself with his hands only for shocks of stabbing pain to radiate up from his palms. Hissing, he toppled onto his side.

He blinked sluggishly, head still spinning as he looked at his hands. As he watched, blood welled up in the web between his left thumb and forefinger, dislodging a shard of glass. He rested his cheek on the tile and looked around. The shards were scattered in a semi-circle around Mireille's feet. He sighed with relief that she hadn't started seizing.

"I might need some help," he said.

She didn't answer.

"Mireille…?" He flipped onto his back, squinting up at her. She was staring straight ahead, face slack. It didn't look like she was even aware of the world around her. "Mireille?"

Nothing.

Nick groaned and got up – slowly this time, leaning against the wall for balance. He shuffled forwards, trying to avoid the glass minefield. Mireille didn't move. He reached out, pinching her sleeve between two relatively blood-free knuckles and tugging. No response. She was like a statue.

Lightning flashed again, thunder clapping at almost the same time. The house shook, windowpanes rattling from the force of it. Nick flinched instinctively, but Mireille didn't even blink. He wondered if there was some condition that made people freeze when lights strobed. It sounded kind of like the opposite of a seizure. Did she have that, too? If she did, he needed to get her away from the windows. Maybe he could tie a dish towel around her head? As his eyes raked over the room, he noticed the drapes were abnormally thick. If he could make one of them into a blindfold, she'd be set.

Or…he could pull them closed. Work smarter; not harder.

There were two sets of windows; one on an adjacent wall and one opposite where they were standing. The latter was probably the priority, seeing as it was the one Mireille was facing, but he figured moving along the walls would be safer in case his vestibular system decided to stop working again. He shuffled as fast as careful baby steps would carry him, leaving a bloody smear on the first drape. Making it to the second set of windows left him feeling like he'd run a marathon.

As soon as he finished, he slid down the wall and rested his hands in his lap as he watched Mireille. He felt a little like time had frozen around him. Thunder boomed again and he reassessed; it felt like time had frozen for Mireille while the rest of the world went on. If it wasn't for the shallow expanding and contracting of her ribcage, he'd believe that was actually the case.

When she moved again, Nick almost jumped out of his skin. Then he lunged forward, scrambling towards her on his hands and knees. "Are you okay? What *was* that?!"

She gaped at him. "What did you do to your hands?"

"Huh?" Nick looked down at his palms. "Oh, I fell on the broken glass. I'm fine. Anyway, you just—"

"Broken glass?" Mireille looked around. Her face fell. "Oh."

"*Oh?!*" Nick echoed. "You just froze like a statue for…I didn't look at the clock, but it felt like a long time!"

"Yeah, sorry about that." She shot him an apologetic look. "I did tell you I have seizures."

He glowered. "I'm not dumb, Se—Mireille. I know what a seizure is. I'm telling you; you weren't moving *at all.*"

"Not all seizures involve spasming." She pulled one of his arms around her shoulders and shifted into a crouch. "Getting up in three…two…"

She stretched the count for as long as he needed to get his feet under him again. As soon as he nodded, she pulled them both up and headed back into the living room. It was tough going, both of them now weakened and wobbling. Finally, they made it to the couch. As Mireille helped Nick sit, he did his best to keep his hands up and away from anything stainable.

"What's up with this?" She mimicked his pose. "Did you hurt your arms?"

"I'm just trying not to get blood on your furniture," he explained.

She smirked, but whatever humor could be found in it was bitter. "Don't worry about it. Thanks to me, my family knows how to get all sorts of bodily fluids out of literally everything." She held up a hand before he could reply. "I'm going to go get the First Aid kit."

"Are you sure that's safe?" Nick asked.

"It's just in the kitchen, and the drapes are closed now. I'll be fine."

He laid back, resting his elbows on his stomach. Rivers of blood crisscrossed his forearms like netting and soaked into his t-shirt, but hopefully it would stay out of the furniture. His parents had raised him to be a polite young man and a good guest, though neither of them had gone into specifics about bleeding politely.

Worrying about Mireille had distracted him from the pain but, unfortunately, he was no longer thus preoccupied. It started as an insistent stinging which quickly intensified into fiery, stabbing agony. Nick groaned, squeezing his eyes shut and throwing his head back against the arm of the couch. He couldn't even manage to look up when he heard the door swing back open and footsteps pad across the carpet towards him.

"Are you okay? That's a stupid question. How badly does it hurt?"

"Have you ever heard of the *gae bolg*?" He murmured.

"No."

Nick hissed when she grabbed his hand, both from pain and surprise.

"Sorry," she said.

"It's alright."

There was a tearing sound, then Mireille started swabbing his skin with what must have been an alcohol wipe. He clenched his teeth, trying to keep from screaming.

"I'm sorry, I'm sorry, I'm sorry," she whispered. "Tell me about the guy bowl."

"*Gae bolg.*" Nick squeezed his eyes shut even tighter, so tightly that he started seeing patterns on the insides of his eyelids. "It's a legendary weapon," he wheezed. "It belonged...to Cu Chulainn, this...Irish mythical hero dude. It was..." He took a few deep breaths. "...this spear-like thing. Except you had to throw it with your foot. And when it hit someone, barbs would come out of it and spread throughout the whole body."

"Sounds horrible," Mireille murmured. After she was finished cleaning his hands as well as she could, she popped open a tube of disinfectant and started to smear it over the wounds. "This stuff is supposed to double as a pain reliever," she said.

"Good," he hissed. "Because right now it feels like I got hit with the *gae bolg*."

"Makes sense," she said. "There are, like, a billion nerve endings in the hand, especially the palms. Makes you wonder why people in books are always doing blood oaths by cutting their palms." She finished off the process with some gauze and a self-adhering bandage wrap.

"Maybe it's on purpose. To...show their commitment or something."

"I guess." She finally released his hands. "How does that feel?"

Nick flexed his fingers and regretted it immediately. "The pain reliever stuff hasn't kicked in yet."

"Well duh, I just put it on. Give it a minute."

Nick risked opening his eyes. His hands were wrapped up mummy-style and his forearms were clean, though he'd been right about leaving some stains on his shirt. Mireille was kneeling next to the couch, backlit by the fire. She stuffed the wrappers and used wipes in a sandwich bag and tossed it across the room. It dropped cleanly into the trash.

"Nice shot," he said.

"Thanks." She shrugged. "When you're stuck at home most of the time, you become pretty good at stuff like that."

Nick nodded slowly. "What else do you do for fun?"

"I read a lot." She stood up and stretched, then sat down in a chair a few feet away. "I go for walks. Oh, and I love swimming."

"I bet," Nick muttered.

"What?"

"Nothing." He cleared his throat. "So, uh, are you reading anything now? *The Great Gatsby* perhaps?"

"I've read that about a hundred times." She smiled softly. "My parents met because of it. They were paired up to do a project on it in high school."

"They both loved it?" He guessed.

"Nope," she laughed. "They both hated it. They bonded over their mutual hatred."

Nick laughed, too. "That's beautiful."

"Right? Anyway, right now I'm actually reading *Divergent*."

"Oh yeah?" Nick craned his neck, but she wasn't holding it. "My brother's girlfriend is obsessed with that series. She dressed up as the main character for Halloween two years in a row. The first year, she just wore black and drew the symbols on her arms in eyeliner, but the next year she had a job so she ordered a bunch of merch off the internet."

"That's cool. Have you ever read it?"

"No." Nick frowned. "I think I have to pee."

Mireille groaned. "Can you hold it? That just took a lot of work to do."

"For a while, probably. Especially if I'm distracted." He looked over at her. "Distract me with something."

"Like what?"

"I don't know. Read to me."

"Seriously?"

"Yeah. What, I don't look like an intellectual?" With a couple dozen agonizingly painful cuts on his hands and a probable concussion from accidentally walking off a cliff, Nick didn't feel like an intellectual.

Fortunately, Mireille seemed to buy it and got up to grab her book, which was still on the floor near the fireplace. She opened to the first page, ignoring the bookmark sticking out near the end. After the next peal of thunder died down, she began. *"Chapter One. There is one mirror in my house. It is behind a sliding panel in the hallway upstairs. Our faction allows me to stand in front of it on the second day of every third month, the day my mother cuts my hair..."*

{ (o.o) }

The silence after a storm is nearly palpable. The world looks different. Not new, even though the colors are more vibrant through the sheen of water that hasn't yet dried. It's a suspenseful peace Everything is standing still, like it's supposed to, but it's hard to trust that it will stay that way.

Nick and Mireille waited on the front steps for Jake to show up. The concrete had dried partially in the sun, but she'd put a towel down for them to sit on anyway. His head didn't hurt as badly and his balance was much improved, but he still had a little bit of a dizzy feeling that came and went. It took him way too long to realize his head only started to spin when he was thinking about Mireille.

Huh, he thought. *Okay.*

He'd never been one for love stories, and romantic subplots just seemed to get in the way. Cam was awesome and he was glad she was dating Jake just because it meant she was around a lot, but he'd never truly understood what the draw of a relationship was. For a while, he'd figured he wasn't "the lovin' kind" as the song goes. And...it wasn't like he'd had some sort of revelation. All those thoughts still made sense to him. There was no switch in his head that was flipped and suddenly he felt like life wasn't worth living without her.

She gave him a kind of…bubbly feeling. Like the carbonation in the champagne his parents let him try on their anniversary. Not overwhelming, just pleasant. He looked at her and thought that maybe a relationship didn't have to be the dramatic, exhausting emotional rollercoaster it looked like in movies. Maybe it could be fun.

"Can I get your number?" He asked before his brain caught up to him. He pressed the heel of his hand to his forehead. "Sorry, I don't know what I was—"

"No, it's okay!" She interrupted. "Sure; you can have my number."

He blinked. "But…wait, how can you have a phone if…?" He trailed off as she dug into the pocket of her fur coat and pulled out a flip phone.

She opened it with a flick of her wrist and held it out. "My parents were totally spoiled by being able to contact my older siblings whenever they felt like it, so they got me one of these and just put duct tape over the screens. The buttons glow, but not enough to bother me."

"Oh." He grabbed his own phone, twisting so his back was to her, his body blocking the light. His thumbs hovered over the keypad. His brain was still a little fuzzy and he couldn't quite remember how to spell her name…

"Ready?" she asked.

Forget it. He typed "Selkie" and moved on. "Alright; go ahead."

He'd barely saved it when the rumble of a motor broke through the uneasy silence of the morning. Mireille stood first, reaching down to help him up. Nick was worried that his weight would be too much for her spindly little arms, but it only took a few seconds to remind him she'd not only lifted his unconscious body onto her ATV, but also more or less carried him into her house. She must have been all muscle, no fat, and minimal tissue. No wonder she had to wear that fur coat everywhere; she had no insulation.

Jake's engine almost drowned out the sound of the wheels crunching over the rocks in front of the lighthouse. Jake parked, twisting the keys out and throwing his legs over the side in one movement. He jogged up to them, as if flaunting the fact that he wasn't bruised over his entire body and possibly concussed. He smiled, but the concern was clear in his eyes.

"Hey buddy, how are you?" He asked in his gentle voice.

"I'm doing alright," Nick replied. He tried to pull away from Mireille and stand on his own but miscalculated how well his balance had improved and almost face-planted in the gravel.

Jake caught him. "I can see that."

Nick stuck his tongue out like the mature individual he was.

Jake rolled his eyes and swept his younger brother into his arms, clearly committed to showing off. He smiled at Mireille. "Thank you for taking care of him."

"It was no big deal," she waved him off.

"It was, though." Jake's smile slipped. "You probably saved his life."

Nick swallowed hard. He hadn't thought of it that way, but all things considered, if he'd been left out in the woods during the storm, battered and concussed... He twisted as carefully as he could to look Mireille in the eyes.

"Thank you," he said.

"Anytime." She blushed and added, "Not that I want you to get hurt again! I just mean—"

"I get it," he said. "No worries."

{ (o.o) }

"Hey," Jake knocked on Nick's door even though it was open. "You ready for this?"

He grinned. "Absolutely!"

"Cool." Jake pointed sternly. "Make sure you're ready by the time Cam gets here. If you make us wait for you to go to the bathroom again, I'll throw you in the ocean."

"Understood." Nick tipped a sarcastic salute.

Jake rolled his eyes and turned to go.

"Hey, wait," Nick pushed himself up on his elbows.

Jake paused mid-step, grabbing the doorframe and swinging himself back around.

"Can, uh – can Mireille come?" Nick's eyes darted around, looking at everything that wasn't his brother. He blushed.

Jake's eyebrows rose. "The selkie?"

"Well, that's not, like, confirmed…" Nick sighed. "Yes."

"Hm…" Jake shifted into a normal standing position, crossing his arms as he considered it. "What if she alerts her people?"

"We can watch her," Nick said. "And if we see her doing something weird, we'll have more evidence for the selkie theory."

"Okay, fine. She can come as long as you stick by her *the whole time*." Jake wiggled his eyebrows. "Like, really close. For science."

Nick flopped back down on the bed and pulled his pillow over his face. "Shuddup."

Jake cackled.

Nick fumbled around for his phone, bringing it under the pillow with him. After all, he was a human and it was just a phone. Why should he have to be the one to move? As it rang, he took a few calming breaths. He told himself not to be nervous; he wanted her to come so they could have *fun*, not so he would be suffering from stage fright the whole time.

"Hello?"

"Hi." His voice squeaked and he coughed to clear his throat. "It's Nick."

"Oh, hi!" She sounded pleasantly surprised. *"How are you feeling?"*

"Good. Much better. I've been cleared for moderate activity, so Jake and girlfriend are taking me ghost hunting at the beach to celebrate."

"Ghost hunting?"

"Yeah! Well, kind of. See, there are reports of ghostly figures near bodies of water in the folklore of, like, every culture imaginable and there has to be some reason – sorry, I can tell you about it later. I was actually wondering if...well, if you wanted to come with us."

For a moment, all he could hear was the buzz of the connection.

"You don't have to if you don't want to—"

"No! No, it sounds fun. I just...are you sure it would be...I mean, do you guys use scanners or...?"

"No, we're old school – it'll be outside, and we try not to use technology in case the EM fields interfere with the creatures. It's going to be seizure friendly." He squeezed his eyes shut and made a face. "That didn't come out right."

"I know what you meant." Mireille sounded like she was smiling. *"Yeah, okay. I'll come. Where is it going to be?"*

"We wanted to go up the coast a little, find a place with fewer people. We can pick you up at the end of the trail. Oh...are you okay to ride in a car at night? Sorry, I didn't even think about that."

"No, it's good. I'll just bring a sleeping mask. That's what I do on road trips with my family."

"Oh. Well, great." He smiled. "So...we'll pick you up in an hour?"

"Alright. See you then."

"Yeah. Bye." Nick lifted the pillow to make sure he actually ended the call. Then he pressed his face into the fabric and squealed. Like a man.

{ (o.o) }

Mireille was already at the end of the trail, a weathered backpack slung over one shoulder. The fur of her ever-present coat fluffed up around the strap. As they approached, she squeezed her eyes shut.

"Kill the lights," Nick ordered.

"Oh shoot!" Jake hissed, flipping the switch. He rolled down his window. "All clear!"

Mireille peeked through her lashes, relaxing when she saw he was telling the truth. She smiled and waved. "Thanks."

Nick slid across the backseat and hopped out, conveniently opening the door for her. He swept an overdramatic bow, and she laughed as she climbed inside. He closed the door and ran around the back of the car. When he got inside, she was just pulling the sleeping mask over her face. It was black with a decal of closed eyelids and lashes in white.

"Hi, I'm Latisha Cameron," Cam said. "Most people call me Cam."

"Why not Latisha?"

Cam shrugged, then pulled a face when she remembered Mireille couldn't see her. "I've been doing sports my whole life, and the coaches always call us by our last names. We fell into the habit, and I guess it just stuck."

"Well, nice to meet you." I'm Mireille." She carefully lifted her hand in the general direction of Cam's voice.

Cam grinned and shook hands. "Nice to meet you, too."

"So, what do you usually do on road trips if you can't see?" Nick asked. "Do you just...talk about stuff?"

Jake snorted. "Wow, Nick. Way to feed into the stereotypes. I think every Boomer within a two-block radius just got a temporary boost to their HP with that one."

"Shut up." Nick kicked the back of his seat.

"Don't make me come back there, you little—" Jake swiped behind him with one arm, which Nick easily avoided by virtue of not having to watch the road.

"Guys, could we at least *try* to get out of the city without swerving onto the sidewalk or into oncoming traffic?" Cam sighed. "Every single time."

"You're one to talk! Isn't it illegal to pass using the shoulder?" Jake fired back.

"That was one time, and the guy was driving way too slowly."

"He was going five miles over the limit!"

"I know, right? Has he never been on the freeway before?"

Nick watched Mireille. She was leaning towards the bickering couple, a wide grin on her face. Even though she couldn't see him, he smiled back. Suddenly, he gasped.

"Hey, we have to stop for road trip snacks!" He batted Jake's head. "Yo! Stop the car!"

"Oh, I thought we weren't going to do that this time because…you know…" Jake's eyes darted to Mireille in the rearview mirror.

Nick leaned closer to her to get in his brother's line of sighed. He leveled a glare at him. "It. Is. Essential."

"It's okay, I can wait in the car."

"No, just wear the mask," Nick said.

She turned towards his voice and dropped her head towards one shoulder – the head-movement equivalent of raising her eyebrows. "*In* the store?"

"Yeah, why not?"

"They're going to think you kidnapped me or something."

"No, they're not," Nick said. "And if they're worried, they can just ask you if you're okay. I'm rolling my eyes, by the way."

Mireille opened her mouth and closed it again a few times. "Well…"

Her hand was smooth and cool in his, like a stone washed up on the beach after millennia of being tossed by the currents. Nick rubbed his thumb along the back of it. Mireille hung on tightly, shuffling closely behind him.

It took a while to get the hang of it. Nick had never been a seeing eye guy before, so he took turns a little too sharply and forgot to mention things like steps or cracks in the floor. When he circled around a stack of 12-packs of Diet Mountain Dew, he heard a thump and a hissed curse. Mireille stopped, nearly tripping him up as she bent to massage her shin.

"Sorry!" Nick whispered.

She shook her head and grinned wryly. "Maybe we should've practiced this before taking it on the road."

"I don't know, people are really into slapstick comedy these days."

"Excuse me, miss?" One of the employees came up to them, shooting Nick suspicious looks. "Are you alright?"

"I'm fine. My friend's helping me around because I'm sensitive to artificial light." She let go of Nick's hand to push up her sleeve. A silver bracelet gleamed in the unnatural brightness. As the employee inspected it, Mireille made a grabby hand in the air until Nick linked their fingers together again.

"What's up with the bracelet?" He asked once the employee had left, semi-satisfied but still giving him the stink eye. He tugged Mireille over to the refrigerated section. "I'm getting one of those iced mocha drinks from Starbee's. What do you want?"

"Any kind of fizzy water with a blue flavor," she shrugged. "It's a medical ID bracelet. I have to wear it anytime I leave the house in case something happens. That way, the EMT's will know what they're dealing with."

"That's pretty brilliant, actually." He handed her a can, which she lifted to her mouth and slurped. "Hey, we have to pay for that first!" He laughed.

"It's not open," she said, tilting it so he could see. "I was just getting the water off the top. Ow." She flinched and pulled away.

"Don't tell me you're sensitive to metal, too," Nick laughed.

"No, I just...I think I cut my lip on the little tab thing."

"Oh, okay."

"Besides, this isn't metal. It's like...aluminum or something."

"Aluminum is metal."

"Depends on your standards."

By the time they got to the beach, the sun had disappeared below the horizon and most of the sky was the star-studded blue-black of night. Only a few waves of amber and gold lingered above the curve of the earth.

A metal gate blocked the parking lot, so Jake pulled over on the side of the road. It was one of those gates that were basically enclosed metal rectangles with bars stretching across the middle. The bars and frame were smooth and cylindrical, which meant they were practically ladders. Very easy to climb over.

"Are we supposed to be doing this?" Mireille asked, hesitating.

"Sure!" Jake shrugged. "It's a public park. The only reason they barricade it at night is because the park rangers don't have a night shift. Or maybe they're trying to stop people from doing drug deals or something."

Mireille shifted from one foot to the other. "Maybe we shouldn't…"

"Don't worry," Cam reassured her. "It's totally safe. We've been here a ton of times before. Anyway, we're just going through the tree line to the shore. It's, like, four hundred yards, tops."

"Yeah, we wouldn't take you deep in the woods for your first hunt," Jake said. He wiggled his eyebrows. "It *is* your first hunt, right?"

"Uh, yeah." Mireille put her hands over her face and groaned.

"Hey," Nick leaned against the bars. "If you really don't want to go, we can hang out here until Jake and Cam get back."

She lowered her hands and bit her lip. "I don't want you to miss out on the fun…"

Nick blew a raspberry and waved her off. "Like Cam said, we come here all the time. I won't be missing anything."

She gave him a small smile. Shaking her head, she laughed a little. "I can't believe I'm doing this."

Jake, Cam, and Nick whooped as Mireille climbed over the fence. She shushed them, almost losing her balance as she twisted around to see if anyone had heard them. Nick put a hand on her shoulder to steady her.

"Alright, let's go!" Jake said in a stage whisper.

The four of them crossed the parking lot, the beams of their flashlights bouncing in front of them. Jake led them to where the trail broke through the tree line. When the wind rustled the branches, Cam made a ghost noise and they all giggled. Something scampered through the underbrush and Nick and Mireille grabbed at each other, colliding in the middle.

"Sorry!" They both hissed.

"Why are we whispering?" Cam whispered.

"Maybe so the ghosts don't hear us?" Mireille suggested.

"Good idea," Jake agreed in a loud stage whisper.

The forest ended abruptly, thick tree cover and undergrowth cutting off at the edge of a stretch of rocky beach. Little rocks ranging from pebbles to the size of a human hand made up the slope down to the water. The shore stretched for about half the length of a football field, curving in a U-shape. The edges of the beach were bordered by small and medium-sized boulders. These bigger rocks formed tiny peninsulas jutting out into the ocean and creating a harbor barely big enough for a dozen rowboats crammed in side-by-side.

"Alright." Jake, who had been leading the way, pivoted and faced the group. "Cam and I will take the left side; you two take the right."

"Remember, ghosts and wild animals can be dangerous. Don't approach either," Cam said.

"Right," Jake agreed. "We'll meet back here in half an hour to compare notes. Oh!" He slid his backpack off one shoulder and hunted around in it for a minute before pulling out a boxy device half the size of his forearm. Handing it to Mireille, he said, "We don't know if ghosts can sense things humans can't, so we didn't want to bring phones. But if you get in trouble, use the Walkie Talkie to call us for help."

She nodded and stuffed it in her own backpack.

"Alright. See you two later."

"Have *fun~*" Cam said in a sing-song voice, winking.

"Uh, okay?" Mireille replied.

Nick hoped it was too dark for her to see him blushing.

They split off towards the right side of the beach. Pebble beaches are like sand beaches in that the ground moves and shifts under your feet. But while grains of sand are pressed down or shuffled aside easily, pebbles rock and resist. Nick stumbled a few times before he adjusted, but it was worth it because Mireille took his elbow to make sure he didn't fall. He wanted to shift to holding her hand, but that would be a little harder to justify.

"Can I ask you something?" Mireille turned to him as they clambered up onto a particularly large rock. The moonlight reflected off the water onto her face, casting silvery waves across her skin.

"Sure; anything."

"Why do you guys go ghost hunting if you're not bringing cameras? Nobody will believe you found anything if you don't have evidence."

"Well, we're not really into it for, like, an academic purpose. We're just curious. And...we're in it for the adventure, I guess." He paused to gauge the distance between one rock and the next, then crouched and sprang across the gap. Turning back to Mireille, he said, "We don't just look for ghosts, either."

"Really?" She scooted back to get a running start before flinging herself over the space after him. One foot slipped off the edge of the rock and she yelped as she lost her balance.

Nick darted forward and grabbed her around the waist as she fell, hauling her back onto the rock. If anyone asked, he would say it was the adrenaline that made his heartbeat quicken under her hand. She tilted her face up, red eyes wide and shimmering like rubies in the moonlight.

"Thanks," she breathed.

"No problem." He swallowed hard and reluctantly pulled away.

They made their way carefully along the peninsula. It was a clear, bright night, and every so often they caught sight of two shadows moving along the peninsula across the bay. The shadows were definitely affected by gravity, which meant they were Jake and Cam. Still, during a ghost hunt anything could be a little spooky.

"Tell me about these water ghosts," Mireille said after a while.

"So, you can't fact check myths and folklore, but when multiple cultures across multiple continents have remarkably similar stories..." he trailed off dramatically.

"Lots of cultures have water ghost myths?"

"Yeah. Not just ghosts, either. There are your mermaid-types and nymphs from places like Ireland, Africa, China, and other places. Then there's this pretty common idea that people who commit suicide via drowning end up as ghosts tied to that specific body of water."

"Oh, wow."

"Right?" Nick was excited and started climbing faster. "I don't know how true they are, but it's a little too coincidental, don't you think?"

"And you really believe all of it?"

"Why not?" He stepped onto a solid-looking boulder only to have it shift under his weight.

Mireille grabbed the back of his shirt and yanked him towards her until he regained his balance. "I don't know, isn't it a little…unrealistic?"

"Is it?" Nick turned to her and smirked. "Says who?"

She shrugged, gesturing widely with one arm. "I don't know. People? Scientists?"

"Isn't *that* weird?" He asked. "Science, as we know it, has been around for what? Five hundred years? Max? Folklore and legends have been around since the beginning of humanity, and yet there's this idea that science is so obviously superior."

"Huh." She paused. "You know, I never thought about it like that."

For a moment, they just stood there, catching their breath. The waves weren't only audible when they broke on the shore. There was a sound as they roiled and rushed within their own domain. It was a deep, powerful sound, yet that water was so tame and shallow compared to even half a mile out. There's something about nature that can't be captured in numbers on paper or even in a computer program. It's an energy, an atmosphere you can only feel when you are physically present in it.

"Let's go over to the other side," Nick suggested.

The two of them scrambled vertically up the small embankment. It was only a few feet of separation, but on the other side the water was much wilder. The wind picked up, and it was like the harbor had been a bubble taming even the air. They couldn't see Jake and Cam's shadows anymore, and the waves were twice or three times as big, crashing deafeningly onto the shore.

Nick spotted a flat boulder a few feet below them and tugged Mireille's arm, pointing it out. They cautiously picked their way down and settled on it, pressing their backs to the uneven rocks behind them. The boulder was big enough that they didn't have to, but they huddled with their shoulders and legs pressed together.

"What do we do now?" Mireille asked. "Just wait?"

"Yep." Nick leaned over so she could hear him better. "It's like birdwatching. You have to be quiet, so the ghosts feel comfortable coming out."

"Does that work?"

"I don't know. It makes sense though, doesn't it?"

She laughed.

They looked out over the shoreline that stretched to the horizon in front of them and the ocean that did the same alongside it and off to their left. The night was so clear that the stars reflected in the water, only the undulating waves indicating that the universe hadn't folded in on itself. Nick tried to keep an eye out for ghosts or whatever they were looking for, but he was much more interested in leaning against Mireille.

Nick wasn't touch-starved; far from it. He came from a very physically affectionate family. So did Cam, who liked to ruffle his hair and give him playful shoves. But touching Mireille, even just arm to arm, felt brand new. His senses were on fire, like he'd never touched a human before. She was soft, even though she had not a single ounce of fat on her body. It was as if he'd been thinking of people as pixels or cardboard and was just realizing that they were made of something more.

She turned to him and suddenly their noses were mere inches apart. Maybe even closer. He knew, logically, that their shoulders should leave plenty of room between their faces, even angled as they were. Maybe it was an example of science failing to assert itself over more common, more inexplicable realities, because there seemed to be no distance at all. Her face took up his whole field of vision. He could see her veins running blue beneath her thin, colorless skin. She was close enough that he could see the texture of it, the indents of her pores.

She was so achingly, incredibly real, and she made him feel real, too. So real he could barely stand it. He could feel the breath in his lungs and the wind on his skin. He was deafened by the roar of the ocean and the blood pounding in his ears. He didn't think about leaning towards her, he just did it. Like it was gravity.

Her lips were soft and a little chapped. He felt them scratch against his mouth and shivered at the honesty of it. Their noses brushed each other as they separated. Nick smiled and she returned the expression, eyes sparkling. He leaned in for another kiss when a bark cut through the night and startled him. He turned around to see a group of seals laying out on the beach. He hadn't even noticed them.

Mireille sighed and rolled her eyes. "Killjoys," she said.

Nick laughed.

{ (o.o) }

Almost a month later, Nick sat on the beach breathing in the salt air. The water was a dull blue, the spray chilling the already-sharp wind. It was a fairly average fall day. He stuck his hands in his pockets and leaned forward, letting his hair fly back from his forehead.

"Hi."

"You made it." Nick opened his eyes and turned to smile up at Mireille.

"Yeah, sorry I'm late." She sat down next to him, handing him one of two drinks she was holding. Fingers as white as bone Chine peeked out from woolen gloves.

"Oh, thanks." The smell of coffee wafted out of the tiny drinking hole, strong and – most importantly – warm. He recognized the travel mug from her kitchen. It was tortoise-shell brown with the words, THE GRAND CANYON ROCKS splashed across it. "You didn't have to do that."

"I wanted to." She took a long sip. "I was making some for myself, anyway, and it seemed rude not to make some for my boyfriend."

The warmth that spread through him had nothing to do with coffee. He scooted closer to her on the sand and put an arm around her. She leaned into his shoulder.

"Does the ocean seem angrier in cold seasons to you?" She asked, eyes drifting to the gray waves.

"Yeah. That, or sluggish. When the ice is thick it seems like it's hibernating, but whenever the water is open in winter it seems to be storming."

"Exactly." She took another drink, then looked down. "Hey, I'm sorry we can't go to a movie or something like normal people."

"Normal is boring." Nick made a face. "Besides, I love coming down here."

"Me too." She tilted her head and smiled up at him. The wind blew her hair back from her face and over his shoulder. "Well, are you ready?"

"Absolutely."

They got up, brushing the sand from their jeans, then started down the beach. Most people either tied their boats at the docks or drove around to boat landings, but Mireille's family didn't do either. A boat lift kept her dad's speedboat from floating away, and the rest of the crafts were kayaks, canoes, and row boats. Whenever they weren't using them, they just hauled them up on shore.

Instead of taking the path back towards the lighthouse, Mireille led Nick over to where the public beach ended, forest encroaching on the waterline. They stomped through the woods, dead leaves crunching underfoot. Skeletal branches reached up towards gray clouds that spread out to the horizon in every direction. There would be rain soon.

Mireille's rowboat was about twenty feet long and ten feet wide at the stern, narrowing to a point at the bow. The inside was coated with black paint. Mireille opened a small chest in the center and pulled out two cushions: one for each of the benches. Nick stood back as she did, studying the design. A replica of *Starry Night* had been painted across each side of the boat. The detail was incredible; it must have taken forever.

"No matter how many times I see that painting, I still can't get over the fact that you did it yourself."

"Yeah, well," Mireille shrugged, the faintest hint of pink spreading across her cheeks. "When you don't have a lot else to do, you find things to keep you busy."

He bit down on his tongue to stop himself from screaming, "Just take the fricking compliMEEEEEE", remembering at the last second that she wouldn't get the reference. Instead, he rolled his eyes and took a sip of his coffee.

"Alright; help me get it out into the water."

"No, no, let me." He stooped to slide off his sneakers and toss them in the bow before rolling up his jeans. "I know you can do it, I just…it's a gentlemanly thing to do, right? It's supposed to be romantic."

"Fiiiiiiiine," she sighed, but she was smiling.

Mireille got in the stern and put a hand on the trolling motor to make sure it stayed as it was; tilted up so it wouldn't scrape along the bottom. As Nick pushed, the sound of the boat sliding through sand made him shudder. It was like teeth scraping across fabric and made him grateful to finally get in the water, even if said water was freezing.

Not literally, of course, but it was cold enough that his calf muscles clenched and a dull ache spread up his legs. That was the problem with water – even at fifty degrees it could cause people to go into shock if they weren't ready for it. At that time of year, the air temperature was inching ever closer to the fifties, and it was usually warmer than the water.

As soon as they were deep enough for Mireille to drop the trolling motor in, Nick shuffled quickly over to the front bench and heaved himself over the side. Curled on the bottom of the boat, he rolled his jeans down and shoved his feet in his shoes before even trying to get up and sit on the bench like a normal person. Mireille laughed at him, and he joined in as she guided them out to sea.

It was easy to exist in nature. In a boat on the ocean, watching the city shrink into the distance, it felt a little like all the responsibilities of life were back there. Under a sky that stretched for thousands of miles, with water underneath them that had been there for thousands of years and would be until the Earth died, things like homework and what to do after graduation didn't seem as urgent as they usually did. Nick took a deep breath and felt something in his chest release. The waves heaved the boat up and down faster, as if nodding in agreement.

"Hey, if there's a zombie apocalypse, we should just take this boat down the coast until we find one of those little islands," he said.

"You think?"

"Yeah, because the zombies probably can't cross the water."

"Right; they're already decomposing, so they'd just fall apart." She nodded thoughtfully. "But what if there are already zombies on the island? Like, someone got bitten and went to the island and infected everyone there."

"Maybe we could clear it out. There wouldn't be that many."

"Yeah, I don't know. My brothers and I always talked about taking a truck and heading for the desert."

Nick tried to take a sip of his coffee, but it splashed out of the hole and went all over his face. Laughing, he wiped it up with his sleeve. "Why the desert?"

"Because the zombies would probably burn." She shrugged. "And even if they didn't, deserts are like wide open spaces. We'd be able to see them coming."

"That's a really good point."

Something wet hit him in the forehead. At first, he thought it was another drop of coffee, but it didn't take long to realize that A) it was cold, and B) it came from above. Nick looked up as the rain started. The boat rocked with a particularly large wave and he flailed, grabbing the side to keep from falling over. Looking back at Mireille, he could see the understanding in her eyes.

"Let's head back," he suggested unnecessarily.

She nodded and worked on turning them around. As she did, a wave hit them broadside and crashed overtop of them. Mireille flung wet hair out of her eyes and squinted. Nick spluttered, curling in on himself to preserve body heat. They were both drenched in minutes as the ocean grew restless and the rain intensified.

Mireille fought with the motor, kicking it up to full speed and leaning her whole body into it to keep them moving in the right direction. Nick turned away from her to check their progress. When he saw the distance between them and the shore, his stomach dropped. Had they moved at all?

Reflexively, he reached into his pocket for his phone. He could call 911, get them to send out someone from the Coast Guard... There was nothing in his pocket. He never brought his phone when he went somewhere with Mireille. True fear pierced him when he realized how helpless he really was.

He turned back, thinking of scooting closer to her and hoping they could share body heat and courage. She was facing him, so she had no idea why his eyes suddenly went wide. He opened his mouth to shout a warning – for whatever good *that* would do – but before he could get a sound out, the wave smashed into the boat and they were in the water.

Nick had thought about what he would do in that situation before. People daydream about strange things. Maybe it's the brain's way of dealing with anxiety. Students think about how they would save everyone if a shooter came into the classroom. Families make facetious plans for the apocalypse. People who live near the water think about how they would grab their loved ones and latch onto the overturned boat, or maybe just put their loved ones on their back and make for shore with all the energy left in their body.

None of Nick's plans were going to work. The waves picked him up and threw him around like a ragdoll. He was sucked under and tossed back up. He thrashed, but he was immediately and completely disoriented. He didn't know where the boat was or what had happened to Mireille.

None of that even came to mind; in fact, he wasn't really thinking at all. There was no despair that his daydreams wouldn't come true or anger at himself for not wearing a life jacket. There was nothing but blind, animal panic as he fought to get some semblance of control over his situation. His fingers and toes already felt like swollen sausages and the sensation was traveling up his arms and legs. They weren't responding to him. It took all his strength just to flop them around and it was definitely not helping.

At first, he thought the thing that slammed into him was another wave, but it was solid. Warm. Alive. His forearm was suddenly caught between teeth, and he discovered a whole new level of panic he hadn't even known existed. He struggled, batting at the creature and twisting to get away. His desperation gave him enough strength to break free, but it wasn't even a minute before he felt the teeth again.

This time they locked onto his shoulder, a position he would barely have been able to fight from if he'd been alert and strong. He spluttered as the creature dragged him through the water, somehow both knowing which direction was which and having the power to get there.

For some reason, it stayed on top of the wild waves instead of diving down to theoretically calmer water. Nick tried to take in as much air as he could, anticipating going under. His brain was spinning, and he was losing consciousness. *No!* He thought, frantically trying to stay awake. *No! I don't want to go yet!* But he was only human, and no amount of willpower would keep the water out of his lungs or the hypothermia out of his bones.

When his knee slammed into a rock, he knew something was wrong. He shouldn't have been able to touch the bottom while his head was above water. He wasn't that big. Unless... It took all his concentration, but he figured out he was in shallow water. Close enough to shore to drag himself up on land if he could only make his body move.

He couldn't make his body move. An exhaustion deeper than he'd ever felt weighed him down. And yet...he *was* moving. No...he was *being* moved. The creature who still had its jaws fastened on his shoulder was pulling him through the water and up onto the beach. On land, he felt like dead weight. Gravity was a boulder pressing down on top of him.

The teeth let go. There was a snuffling and something like a bark. Something warm pressed against his face. Something with whiskers. Nick's head lolled to the side. His eyes, barely open, fixed on the creature as it pulled back. *A seal...?* If he didn't know better, he'd have thought it looked worried.

Not that he was able to do much thinking before his conscious mind finally gave in.

{ (o.o) }

Nick wasn't sure if he'd been unaware of the pain when he was unconscious or if his mind just hadn't made a note of it, but waking up was accompanied by a sudden sharp ache in his...everything.

He opened his eyes to a white room with a white ceiling. He was lying on a white bed with white sheets and wearing a white gown. There was a steady beeping from his left. He looked over and gazed listlessly at one of the only spots of color in the room; a black heart monitor with glowing green and red readings. His brain felt like a whole person he was trying to drag out of bed; not necessarily resisting, but not alert or active, either.

A creak from his right shifted his attention and he rolled his head over to check it out. On the other side of an IV stand was a chair. Mireille was sitting in it, knees pulled up in front of her. She had a sleeping mask on and headphones that were attached to a smartphone which definitely wasn't hers. He craned his neck to check out the screen, but it was dark.

Lifting his arm took all the energy he had in his body, and he *just* managed to bat at her leg. She startled, one hand reaching for her mask before she remembered where she was. She tugged the headphones out of her ears, swinging her legs onto the floor and leaning forward. Her hands shot out towards the bed, feeling around for him. Nick caught her hand in his and squeezed.

"You're awake," she said.

"Yeah." His voice was rough and scraped along his throat. He coughed. "Did you get a new phone?"

"My sister's. She has a bunch of audio books. How are you feeling?" She felt along his arm to his face and pressed the back of her hand to his forehead. "You don't feel like you have a fever. You were out for a long time, though. How are you feeling?"

He tried to laugh at her flustered speech, but it came out as a cough. "Is there any water in here?"

She touched her mask. "I don't know."

Groaning, he swung his head around, taking stock of the room. "There's a tray table with a pitcher and some cups. It's, like, a foot to your left."

Mireille got up and cautiously moved left, hands held out in front of her. It took her a minute to find the table, then another to feel around until she found the pitcher and cup. Some water splashed on the tray when she tried to pour it, but it was a mostly successful endeavor.

As she shuffled back over, Nick noticed a remote and figured out how to angle himself up. She sat back down, and he lifted the cup to his lips. He told himself to take it easy. Chugging wasn't supposed to be good for digestion.

He downed the whole cup in one gulp.

The water hit his stomach hard and he grimaced as it cramped immediately. Apparently, he'd been unconscious long enough that it was empty.

"So," Mireille prompted. "How are you feeling?"

"I'm alright." After all the time she'd spent waiting, it was probably an underwhelming answer. Still, he was too exhausted to think up something better. "What happened?"

"What's the last thing you remember?"

He closed his eyes and concentrated. It was there, hovering like a plotline built on suspension of disbelief. If he didn't look too closely at it, he could push it aside and move on. Unfortunately, he'd heard that refusing to process events could be unhealthy in the long run. He sat still and remembered.

"I think…there was a seal," he said, opening his eyes. "The boat tipped over and a seal dragged me to shore."

Mireille's forehead creased and she shook her head. "No…there was no seal. You must have hit your head when the boat flipped. *I* was the one who swam us both in."

"What?" He frowned at her even though she couldn't see him.

She shrugged, face turning neutral.

Nick trusted her, but…the memory of the water, the way he was absolutely powerless against enormous, angry waves, was still pulsing like an open wound in his mind. It was terrifying; he hadn't been able to *think* let alone look for Mireille. Yet she'd not only gotten her bearings, but found him *and* gotten them both to shore?

"Are *you* okay?" he asked. "The water was freezing."

She nodded. "I was fine; I had my coat. You were hypothermic when the ambulance showed up, though."

Nick looked at the coat, which was draped over the back of her chair and still dripping on the floor. "So, you swam through a storm weighed down by a waterlogged coat and dragging a person behind you?"

She shrugged. "The doctors said it was probably an adrenaline rush."

"Right." Of course it was. What was he thinking? He'd hit his head and that dumb theory about her being a selkie had gotten mixed up with whatever his body remembered about the rescue. Why was he interrogating her after she'd saved his life?

"Thank you," he added belatedly. "You're my hero. Again."

She smiled, posture relaxing. "I'm glad I could be," she said. "I don't know what I'd..." She turned her head away and cleared her throat. "I don't know what I'd do if I lost you."

The last of his suspicions melted away under the warmth of his feelings for her. He took her hand. "This might just be the Knight in Shining Armor effect, but I think I love you."

Those words had terrified him for weeks. He'd wanted to tell her before but didn't want to ruin what they had or make her feel like he was pressuring her. Then he'd almost died. He could've been dead. Every second for the rest of his life would be bonus time. And what better way to use bonus time than by taking risks for the things that matter?

She squeezed his hand. "I love you, too."

Nick grinned and pulled as hard as he could. "Come up here."

"Nick!" She giggled. "No, I can't – you're supposed to be re-covering."

"Yeah, so are you, probably."

She gave in and let him pull her up on the bed. He put an arm around her shoulders as she curled into his side. He touched noses with her as a heads-up before going in for a kiss.

"I love you," he said again.

She sighed happily. Suddenly, she sat up and reached over towards the chair where she'd been sitting. His arms already felt empty without her.

"What are you doing?"

"Nothing, just..." She settled back down and put her sister's phone on his chest. "We have a lot of books. I can't read to you right now because of the lights and you can't read to me because you probably have a concussion, so..."

"Oh, good idea." He swiped open the phone to reveal a truly impressive selection of audiobooks. "How about *The Little Mermaid*?"

She snorted. "No."

"Why not?"

"Pick something else."

"I think it would be appropriate."

"I want to listen to a murder mystery."

"That's not very romantic."

"It could be." She wrapped an arm around him gently. "If I get scared, I might have to hang onto you."

"Hm." He rested his cheek against her hair. "I guess I could go for that."

About the Author

K. R. VANDERPORT

Katherine Rose Vanderport is the author of the novel *Maggie and Elliot Defy Gravity* and the poetry collection *Try on My Glasses*. She lives in Northern Minnesota with her cat, Jules Purrne. Besides reading and writing, she likes to dance, drink coffee, and go exploring.